D1505366

THE TRIAL OF
Mary Lou

Published by:
Harbour Books
147 Armstrong
Claremont, CA 91711

Library of Congress Cataloging-in-Publication Data

Carter, Ron, 1932-
    The Trial of Mary Lou : The funniest court story ever recorded
    Ron Carter
        p.   cm. -- (The settlement trilogy : v. 1)
        ISBN 0-9643672-5-4 (alk. paper)
        I. Title.   II. Series.
PS3553.A7833175   1996
813 .54--DC20   96-3111
                                                                       CIP

hardcover: ISBN 0-9643672-5-4

Publication Director: Barbara Ciletti
Design and production: Graphic Relations
Cover illustration: Greg Michaels
Printing: Publishers Press, Salt Lake City, Utah

10 9 8 7 6 5 4 3 2 1

THE TRIAL OF
Mary Lou
An American Folktale

VOL. I THE SETTLEMENT TRILOGY

RON CARTER

HARBOUR BOOKS
CLAREMONT, CA

1

"O MERCY, MERCY ME!" MARY LOU Hubbard clapped her small, delicate hands over her mouth as her huge violet-blue eyes widened.

"Papa ain't going to like this."

Standing stock still on the smooth, weathered planks of the front porch of the ancient log cabin with the mud chinking that had been the Hubbard home for more than thirty years, she watched the man laboring with the oars in the rowboat. He worked steadily across the broad, green-brown waters of the Snake River towards the Hubbard boat landing sixty yards down the gentle incline from the cabin to the river bank.

The tall pine trees that surrounded the house and filled the gap between house and river stood unmoving, shining deep emerald green in the pure, still, clean, warm June air and a hush made the single warbling call of a meadowlark sparkle like crystal.

Dropping her hands, she confirmed, "That there is Corvis Lumley coming in that boat as sure as sure, and he ain't up to no good."

She remembered vividly some of the visits Corvis Lumley had made in past years while the family was gone from home visiting, or into the Settlement. He let the milk cow out of the barn and scattered the pigs into the trees and when she and Papa got home, it took them an hour to round them up and get them penned again.

'Course then Papa had to work back across the river to the Montana side next time he saw old Lumley drive his rattletrap Model A Ford pickup to town, and Papa snuck five pounds of salt into Lumley's moonshine still, and when old Lumley sold off that batch to some of his customers before he found out, he like to got himself killed, particularly by his Idaho customers who had rowed the river in a rainstorm at night to get a couple of jugs.

So Lumley had to row back across to the Idaho side next time he saw Papa and Mary Lou drive away in *their* old rattletrap Model A Ford pickup and slip a little croton oil into the well, and it gave Papa and Mary Lou the skitters for about three days until Papa figured it out, and they had to carry water from the creek for more than a week while the croton oil settled out of the well.

So Papa had to row back to the Montana side next time old Lumley left for town, and Papa took a coyote pup he'd caught a few days earlier and stuffed it into Lumley's chicken coop for ten minutes. The pup was more scared than the hens, but the laying hens raised a squawk that could be heard plumb to Missoula and then they went into a moult and shed all their feathers and quit laying eggs for a month. The ruckus the hens raised scared the coyote pup so bad Papa couldn't get him out from under the porch for six weeks, and even after that, when the pup saw a chicken in the yard he became a gray streak heading for the comparative safety of the darkness under the house.

And this had been going on two or three times a year for all of Mary Lou's seventeen years, as long as she could remember. It started even before Mama died twelve years ago and her four older brothers come full-growed men and took themselves a wife and left home.

Mary Lou spun with the agility of a deer and her bare feet scarcely touched the planks as she dashed to the far end of the porch and looked up through the pines, desperately hoping Papa hadn't yet disappeared around the bend. But all she saw was the fine grains of dust settling in the bright sunlight, into the ruts of the ancient, hard dirt road where the old rusty pickup had passed.

She crept back to the center of the porch and looked down at the boat landing and watched as Lumley turned around in the boat to come into the wharf frontwards, so he could see if anything was moving.

Carefully Mary Lou backed up until she felt the back hem of her old, faded, full- length gingham dress touch the door, and she reached behind herself and lifted the latch and backed into the kitchen. In a trice she was at the open window, watching Lumley come the last thirty yards cautiously, his eyes covering the house and the yard and the barn for any movement. It was clear he thought the place was deserted.

Mary Lou pursed her mouth and then slowly reached above the window and quietly lifted the familiar, old, worn family Winchester .30-30 from its pegs and jacked a shell into the firing chamber and waited. Maybe Lumley would turn around on his own accord and leave the place alone. But he continued, stroking more strongly with his left oar against the slow current of the broad river, to keep coming in a straight line.

When he was thirty feet from the wharf, Mary Lou rested the Winchester over the window sill and waited just a few more seconds. When he was twenty feet from the wharf and she knew he meant to come right on up to the place, she took rapid aim and triggered the first cracking shot. Then within the next five seconds she levered and fired five more blasting shots from the smoking rifle, the yellow, empty cartridge casings jangling and rattling on the kitchen floor.

Corvis Lumley heard the first .30 caliber slug hit the bottom of his rowboat geometrically between his spread feet, and the sing of the bullet, and the sound of the rifle crack all at the same instant. His head dropped forward and he was absolutely transfixed, rooted to the spot as he watched a twelve-inch, .30-caliber geyser start to swamp the bottom of the boat. Then, instantly, his head jerking up and down with each one, five more whacks and blasts and five more holes and five more .30 caliber, twelve-inch geysers, all within one hand span, right between his feet. Involuntarily he threw his feet further apart, against the sides of the boat, and then jerked his head up to see who was shooting.

He saw a huge cloud of white smoke hanging in front of the

kitchen window in the still sunlight, from the old, black powder shells, and then the kitchen door opened and he clearly saw Mary Lou stride onto the porch, her long, golden hair woven into one braid down the length of her back, standing her full five feet two inches, puffing her 103 pounds to look bigger and more ferocious, the Winchester clutched in her hands, cocked, ready.

With great haste Corvis Lumley buried his left oar in the water, and by making twelve deep strokes in four seconds, he was headed back towards Montana. Once the bow of the boat came on course, he began stroking both oars with great vigor.

Mary Lou watched for a moment, then lowered the rifle and stood it against the kitchen door frame, never taking her eyes from Lumley. The turning of the boat slowed her. Never had she seen twelve oar strokes as deep as those, in four seconds. The water fairly roiled as Lumley turned the boat.

Then her forehead furrowed in disbelief as she watched him begin pulling for home. The oars were hitting the water in perfect rhythm, thirty strokes to the minute. She counted them. On the river, the rings from oar dips usually disappeared pretty fast in the current, but these rings were still spreading for nearly a minute after Lumley's oar blades buried in the water, and they were close enough that they were overlapping. Even at the Fourth of July celebration when they had boat races and the young mountaineers from all around the settlement gathered to show off, no one had ever come close to what Lumley was doing with his oars.

Mary Lou skipped off the porch and her bare feet made little puffs of dust on the worn path down to the boat landing as she watched Lumley continue across the river. The boat settled lower and lower in the water and Lumley pulled faster and harder on the oars, and suddenly Mary Lou found herself quietly cheering him on.

"Come on, Lumley, pull, you can make it before she sinks!"

But Lumley didn't.

Sixty feet from the Montana bank he made his last oar stroke with the oar locks awash, and the boat sank out from under him. He remained seated on the plank seat until his chin went under water before he began to swim for shore.

Mary Lou watched long enough to be sure he dragged himself

through the willows along the bank, onto the flats where the sagebrush claimed the land, and she watched him stand up and turn to face the Idaho side.

He raised one fist, then both, in defiance, while the water sloshed and splattered all around him, and she could hear his vehement roar clear across the 120 yards of the rolling river.

"Now you've done it. You'll pay for this! You'll pay! By cracky, you've done it! You coulda kilt me! I'm getting the law. You'll pay!"

"My my my, carrying on so, what is the matter with that man?" Mary Lou muttered to herself as she walked back up the path to the porch, where she picked up the Winchester. She entered the kitchen and opened the table drawer where the bullets were kept, and quickly rammed six fresh cartridges into the loading port before replacing the rifle on its pegs.

2

"YOUR MORNING MAIL, SIR." ALFRED Atchley Ambrose Humble set the silver tray down on the side of the huge, dark oak desk, his hand held rigid, nose high. His tall, slender, rather rawboned frame and hawkish face lent a slight "Ichabod" aura to his bearing, which was otherwise thoroughly British.

Governor Cornelius Potts leaned forward in his chair and unceremoniously reached around to scratch his backside, his eyes running over the spread of mail on the silver platter. His own short, square, corpulent self, with his thinning hair and ruddy, round, loose-jowled face left much to be desired by way of lending physical attractiveness to the office of governor. In an effort to acquire someone with qualities that would offset his own rough, rudimentary beginnings that included habits of scratching his behind, belching on occasion, and hugging old, bearded, smelly miners and ranchers that came to visit him from time to time, Governor Potts had hired Humble to be his personal secretary. By any fair man's standards, Humble was a model of propriety and proper English, although he was a naturalized American, having emigrated some ten years earlier, shortly after World War I.

The top letter on the stack instantly caught Potts' eye. He checked the fancy scroll of the return address as he spoke.

"Al, what's Buggs up to now?"

"Beg your pardon, sir, it is not my custom to read official mail intended for . ."

"Come on, Al. What's it say?"

"Governor Cuthbert Buggs has written to inform you that a citizen of this state has assaulted a citizen of his state with a rifle. He intends that you try that citizen in this state for attempted murder, or that you deliver said citizen to his state for trial. But a trial there must be."

A sly smile lifted one side of Potts' mouth and he said, "Old Buggs just won't quit until he gets even, will he?"

"Apparently that is correct, sir."

Getting even had become an obsession for Governor Buggs of Montana, a handsome, dashing six-footer, over a year ago, when two old, bearded, grizzled, Idaho hard-rock miners ventured onto an island about three-quarters of a mile long and half a mile wide in the middle of the Snake River, where the river served as the border between Idaho and Montana. They were prospecting for gold. Despite the hoots and side-splitting laughter of other old miners who found out about it, they hit a huge pocket of gold nuggets in a rocky outcrop just about dead center on the island. They staked their claim and two weeks later showed up at the Lemhi County seat in Idaho to file it in the state records.

When they finished, they dumped a huge leather bag of pure gold nuggets, some the size of chicken eggs, on the assayer's table, and the news spread like wildfire. Within one day it reached Buggs. Quickly he got out a map and called in his secretary of state.

"Is that island Montana territory or Idaho territory?"

"I'll get the attorney general."

When the Attorney General arrived, he stroked his chin and said, "That depends on where the meander line is in the river, at that point. I'll get the state surveyor."

When the state surveyor arrived, he pulled out his ever-present scaling ruler and laid it on the map and said, "Can't rightly tell. It's too close to call. I'll have to send out a survey team."

"Do it," said Buggs, "now. Some of those nuggets are the size of oranges."

The news of the Montana survey team got back to Potts the day after they left Helena, headed for the Snake River in Ford sedans as far as they could go, then on horseback, leading pack horses.

"Get the best survey team you can find," Potts demanded of his state surveyor, "now. Some of those nuggets are as big as grapefruit. I'm not about to let that gold wind up in Buggs' hands."

The two survey teams, four men each, tied their rowboats up at the island at the same time, on opposite sides, and met in the middle. For half a day they eyed each other and walked around each other stiff-legged like fighting roosters as they set up their equipment and began their surveys to determine whether the claim was an Idaho claim or a Montana claim.

All four men on both teams, being hard-rock miners themselves, had included in their packed provisions two old crock jugs for each team. As the day wore on and the heat of the late May sun bore down, they decided there was no reason they couldn't be friendly, so they sat down together and talked about how their surveys were coming, and compared a few notes, and then whatwith the heat and all, they allowed they would do better if they cracked open a jug or two and had a snort. Whatever their differences might be, there are not two old hard-rock miners in the world who disagree on that as standard survey procedure.

Two jugs later they finished their surveys and decided they could surely row back to their separate states by the light of a full moon or two.

When the state land office in Montana plotted the survey of the Montana team, the island was located eight miles south and a little west of Yellowstone Falls in Wyoming. When the state land office in Idaho plotted the survey of the Idaho team, the island was located twenty-one miles south of the Canadian border, north of Lake Pend Oreille, Idaho. By specific gubernatorial order of both Potts and Buggs, jugs were banned from provisions of official state survey teams forever.

Buggs and Potts fussed and fumed for a while, but neither did much about it, and the gold strike remained the property of the two Idaho miners. Two months later the miners returned to sell their gold and were crestfallen.

"That goldanged vein was just a pocket. She plumb petered out. Ain't no vein at all. Just that one pocket. Yes sir, we even dynamited, and we couldn't find no showing at all of yella. Just that one pocket."

And the two old miners abandoned their claim.

Potts thought about that for a day or two and then called Buggs on the telephone.

"I been thinking about that island, Gov. Maybe I was a little tough. Neighbors ought to be neighbors. Tell you what. You want the claim, we'll sell you whatever mineral rights this state has to the island for just about nothin'. Well, maybe five thousand bucks or so, you know, just to make it look right. No further questions asked." Two days later the five thousand bucks arrived in Potts' office and the deed to the mineral rights was sent to Buggs.

A month later Buggs learned it was worthless. He raved and ranted for two days, but pride would not allow him to let on he had been swindled, so he swore he would find a way to even things out, and he waited, the rancor growing inside.

Governor Potts read the three-page letter twice while Humble stood quietly by, poised, waiting in silence.

"Yeah, I think old Buggs means to get even. He's demanding that this Hubbard girl, whoever she is, be tried for attempted murder or he's going to start extradition proceedings and likely get the feds involved. Al, you ever heard of a town over on the Snake River referred to as just 'the Settlement'?"

"No sir. Nothing by that name."

"I been over through that part of the state a time or two myself, but I don't recall a town or settlement by that name either. I wonder where it is."

"Shall I find out, sir?"

"Naw, let me make a call or two."

Five minutes later Potts leaned back in his chair. "It's in Lemhi County, somewhere north of Leadore. Right smack in the middle of the Bitterroot Mountains, looking down on the Snake River. Post office lists it as an RFD, but not a town. They got a smattering of names out in that country and when they get a big enough pile of mail a guy goes in there for a couple weeks on horseback and delivers it. From what the post office told me, the citizenry over there didn't know World War I was over until 1922. Last year, in 1930, they heard about the stock market crash of '29 and that the country was in trouble and good men in the cities were struggling to earn thirty bucks a month. Folk from the Settlement wondered where they could go to earn thirty hard Yankee dollars in a month."

Potts tipped his head backwards and scrooched his face into a prune while he scratched his ample, sagging jowls.

"Tell you what, Al. Let me think on this one. If old Buggs gets one of my people over there, he'll pop 'em in the clink just to get even with me. That just won't do. Let me think about it for a while."

For two hours Governor Cornelius Potts went about his usual duties, occasionally stopping to run his hand through his hair, or scratch, as he thought. He pulled and pushed at the problem and slowly it began to settle in his mind. When it was clear what he should do, he whanged on the bell on his desk and instantly Humble appeared, looking impeccable as always.

"Al, I think I got it. Now listen. Here's what we do. Lemhi County has only one part time county attorney who never saw the inside of a law school, and anyway they sure can't send him over on the river to try an attempted murder case and leave the county unattended. So I'm going to get the attorney general to send over the brightest lawyer on his staff, no matter who he is, to represent the State of Idaho in the prosecution of this case. Now the way I figger it, that ought to impress Buggs. But if I do that, and the trial goes on before a regular district judge, they just might convict this Hubbard girl, and that ain't going to happen. If she took a shot at that Lumley guy from Montana, he probably had it coming, so I ain't going to have her get convicted for it. Al, you trackin' with all this?"

"Uh, yes sir. I'm - uh - trackin'." Humble set his teeth in pain at the forced use of the vernacular.

"So how do I keep her from getting convicted? I don't send in the regular district judge! That's how I do it. Partly because he don't get over that direction more than once every couple of years anyhow, and partly because he wouldn't know what to do with those back-country folk if he did."

Potts paused to get his thoughts organized. "But I do! I know those people. By cracky, I come from a bunch just like that. So I'm going to appoint one of them to be the district judge. Special appointment. Try just this one case. Chances are there hasn't been a trial for attempted murder over there in the history of the state. Someone gets plugged out in those kind of places, they usually have it coming and nobody complains."

Potts stood and unceremoniously rubbed his itchy nose for a minute before continuing.

"So get the attorney general down here and see if the post office department can get me the name of the man who has got the most mail delivered to him over near the Settlement during the past couple of years. Then get me a copy of the state constitution, and one of those black robes judges wear when they're judging."

"Yes sir, at once sir. Er, sir, may I inquire? I understand the part about the attorney general and the black robes of justice. But what is the purpose of the name of the man who has received the most mail, and the copy of the constitution?"

"The man who has received the most mail is likely the man who can read best over there, and I figure to send him a copy of the constitution along with a letter outlining what he's supposed to do and authorizing him to do it. I figger if he'll puzzle over the constitution just a little, he'll at least get a glimmer of an idea about due process and the basic rules about jury trials and such."

"Oh. Of course sir. Very good sir. I'll set about it at once."

3

"HUGH FITZGERALD IS THE MAN."

The attorney general, Hector Dingel, turned to his administrative assistant who had just delivered Potts' request.

"The best I got. Graduated from high school at age fifteen and from Harvard College and Harvard Law School a month ago at the same time at age twenty. Brilliant. Took this job to see the west for a year before he starts teaching at Harvard. Got here week before last. Get him down here right now."

A minute later, Hugh Fitzgerald raised his crossed legs off his desk and swung his feet to the floor, his youthful, handsome, blue eyed, smooth cheeked face puckered in question.

"Dingel wants me for what?"

"Special assignment. Over on the Montana border. I don't know all about it, only that it involves an attempted murder charge."

Instantly Hugh rose to his full five feet seven inches and shrugged his coat onto his 130 pound frame, his eyes glistening. He took a moment to be certain enough white shirt cuff protruded from the end of each sleeve and his celluloid collar was exactly straight before following the administrative assistant out of the hole-in-the-wall office and down the huge marble corridor, past the rotunda of the state capitol building that backs onto State Street. They walked through the large doors with ATTORNEY GENERAL printed on the frosted glass.

"Good morning, Fitzgerald," Dingel said, gesturing towards a chair facing his large desk.

"Good morning," Hugh replied, focused, tense. "Do I understand I am being assigned to a case?"

"True. The governor has asked for a man of your qualifications for a special assignment on the east side of the state. You're to go there as soon as you can and prepare to prosecute an attempted murder case."

"Where?" Excitement was rising in Hugh.

"The Settlement. Seems to be a place we can't find on our maps, but we can get you within three or four miles of it. From there, you'll just have to hunt for it. Right on the Snake River, above Leadore."

Hugh nearly gasped with excitement. The frontier! "Is Leadore a town?"

"Sort of. More of a mine. But the Settlement is somewhere north of it. Quite a ways."

"How do I get there?"

"To Pocatello on the train, then north past Leadore in an automobile until the road ends, then the last fifty five or sixty miles by horseback."

Fitzgerald's eyes sparkled. Raw wilderness at last! "Who will be the judge?"

"Don't know yet. Someone appointed by Potts from the local gentry over there."

Hugh pursed his mouth for a moment. "And who will be the defense counsel?"

"Same. Appointed from the locals over there."

"Where is the courthouse?"

"There isn't one. You'll just have to find the Settlement and let the judge pick the place. Might be out in the open."

Fitzgerald glowed. Untutored judge, unlearned defense attorney, no court house. Justice being brought to the pure and humble in the primal setting of some adobe that has housed the pioneer, the adventurer, the true patriots of the American dream!

"Who is the man I am prosecuting?" Visions of an unkempt,

dirty, rotten, smelly, contemptible, drunk skunk who had stuck a knife in someone's back flitted through his brain.

"Mary Lou Hubbard. Seventeen years old. That's all I know."

Hugh batted his eyes and shook his head as Dingel's description collided with his mental image of the defendant. "Mary Lou Hubbard?!? He is a she?"

"Right. The alleged victim is a Montana citizen, fella by the name of Corvis Lumley."

"Come on, Dingel," Hugh blurted. "You got it backwards. That filthy villain Lumley tried to murder Mary Lou."

"That's not what the message says. 'Course you get there and find out you're right, prosecute Lumley. In the meantime, the defendant is Mary Lou Hubbard."

"What do I take with me?"

"A change or two of clothes. A little money we'll give you. That's about it."

"Do I go armed?"

Dingel's forehead wrinkled in puzzlement. "Armed? What for?

"Savages."

"You mean Indians?"

"Yes."

"No." Dingel reached to scratch his chin while he puzzled on what Hugh was seeing in this assignment.

"When do I leave?"

"5:15 train east in the morning. Can you be ready?"

"Absolutely. I'd better get to my apartment and get packed. And I must write a letter home to Boston."

He hastily walked out the door and back to his office, remaining long enough to put his desk in order. Then he trotted the three blocks east on Eighth Street to his small second-story apartment in the attic of old Widow Fangenwaller's home, and for nearly an hour sat with pen in hand, eyes aglow and tongue alternately grasped between his teeth, then retreated into a lump inside his pursed mouth as he labored.

He composed a work of art describing his assignment into the wild, villain-and- savage infested, unmapped regions to the north that put his mother into three days of fainting spells when she received it a week later.

4

ABNER PLUM STOPPED IN HIS TRACKS. "Well, tarnation," he muttered under his breath. "She's stoppin' here?"

The River Belle was owned by the Big Sky Pie Mining Company and was one of the two paddlewheelers used to run gold ore from their mine up around Goldsboro down the river to the smelter just below Leadore. She stopped at the settlement rarely, usually only in the direst emergency, like the time the captain got drunk and ran her onto some rocks and had to beach her at the Settlement for two days while he sobered up and they got the hole fixed well enough for her to make it back to Leadore.

"Something bad has happened. I can feel it in my bones."

Abner was always the first to know when something bad had happened because he faced all of life's surprises knowing something bad had happened and he always said so. After a while people didn't notice so much that a lot of the time he was wrong in his mournful predictions; they only remembered that he had predicted most of the local catastrophes over the last thirty years while he ran the place in the Settlement.

"The place" was the remains of the old Cataldo mission chapel, built of adobe mud bricks in the 1600s when the Spanish came to claim the territory for the Spanish Crown. The Spanish got run out by the French and the French by the Nez Perce Indians and the Indians by the US Cavalry, and the US Cavalry by civilization. The old mission had been plundered by each God-inspired Christian group after the Spanish. Cannon and rifle shot pitted the walls on all four sides. The graceful old Spanish bell tower had been shot away along with most of the decorative architecture above the windows and along the roof line. The French had blown the huge entry doors to kindling with a keg of powder to route the priest and some of his parish. When the cavalry ran the Indians out, they put huge sheet iron shutters on all windows at ground level, on hinges so they could be closed during Indian attack.

After each stage of its destruction, those remaining at the Settlement had done only what was necessary to adapt the aging structure to their own immediate needs. Repairs were half-hearted or nonexistent. The huge entry had been plugged with rough planking after the big doors were blown, except for one door built on one side for getting into the front of the building.

With the Indian threat long past, the old iron battle shutters hung at odd angles, pitted by rust and neglect. Partitions had been set up inside the building to accommodate need.

Abner now ran what would be called a general store, post office, and news and gossip business out of the front door. At the back of the building, Maudie ran a laundry, watering stop, overnight bed for travelers, sewing shop, first aid station, midwife service and all-round woman's stop out of one large, cluttered room. A doorway had been cut through the back wall to accommodate it, and a door frame and door built which didn't quite fit the hole the sledgehammers made, so the leaks had been stuffed with rags and dried grass.

Out of the west side of the building a person could buy a little hay and grain for animals when old man Gibbons could be found; he was often snoozing in a stall at the livery barn he ran, not far from the blacksmith shop. If Gibbons was gone, you bought grain from Abner and he dropped whatever he got paid into a Prince Albert tobacco can that was left on the barrel by the door.

The second floor of the building was just one huge room that had been converted to storage for pelts brought in by trappers. At the end of each season the pelts had been hauled downstream to Leadore in an old plank barge and sold, each trapper coming back to the place in the fall to collect his share of the price, according to his receipt. The fur trade slowed to just a trickle before 1900, then stopped altogether, leaving the second floor a gigantic, empty room, with strong aromas reminiscent of the time furs had been stored in the heat until late in the spring season.

Three hundred years of harsh winters and hot, dry summers had eroded much of the adobe, particularly around the bullet and cannon shot craters, leaving the old building weather stained, pockmarked, dilapidated.

The place stood in the center of the Settlement. Bare dirt ran in all directions for a hundred yards, interrupted by just the blacksmith shack where guns and traps, horseshoes, wagon wheels and Model A and Model T Fords could be repaired by Homer Waller, who slept by the forge, and old man Gibbons' livery, where a passing trapper or miner could get his horse or mule put up for the night. Not one building or plank in the Settlement had ever felt the stroke of a paintbrush. Viewed as a whole, the Settlement looked tired and colorless and ramshackle and eternal.

Abner watched as the empty paddlewheeler labored up to the boat dock and slowed, the wheels turning only enough to hold the boat still in the water while one of the crew jumped to the wooden dock and started up the slight incline towards the Settlement at a trot, a box wrapped in brown paper tucked under one arm.

"Yep, something's wrong," Abner repeated and started from the place down towards the approaching boat hand at a rapid walk, his small, wiry, bowlegged frame swaying slightly from side to side with each step as the boat hand puffed up to him.

"Abner, got a package here for Clyde Dinwoody, emergency, from the governor! Come by special messenger to the smelter and he said we got to deliver it right away. Paid ten hard American dollars for us to do it. Where's Clyde at?"

"I reckon out on his diggins, still foolin' around with that experiment of his. What you got there?"

The boat hand thrust the package to Abner. "Don't know. Strict orders was to not open it. We can't wait so you get her on to Clyde right now."

Abner grasped the box in both hands and immediately shook it, which resulted only in silence. The boat hand was halfway back to the River Belle before Abner started back to the place, face drawn into a road map of wrinkles while he puzzled at what in thunderation the governor could want with Clyde Dinwoody.

Clyde was a quiet one, had been all his life. Fairly good-sized, usually pleasant, a bachelor, with a square face that looked content most of the time, topped by a thatch of brown hair that had most of the qualities of good bailing wire. He seemed satisfied to sit on his diggins - a cabin and a little clearing a mile and a half west of town - and receive an installment of mail once a month from the university, telling him how to grow some kind of grain in these parts, wild.

He got the idea from a 1912 seed catalog he found in the corner of Maudie's store one day, and a month later got up the gumption to write the univesity about it. It took him and Abner two days to get the letter just so, and ever since they mailed it, Clyde had been receiving university letters once a month, - more mail than anyone for a hundred miles. They sometimes got delivered three or four at a time, depending on how often the mail got in. The first letter said others would follow.

Then the envelopes got bigger and with each letter there was a sample of seed, each just a little different than the last, with instructions. No need for water or nothing, just throw her down and she comes up and bears grain. Abner reckoned it was a dang nuisance, delivering those letters over the past year, and all for nothing because "any fool knows you ain't going to grow no grain up here in these pines."

"Sure enough," said Abner once he got his glasses from the store, "it's from the governor, and it says URGENT."

He put his glasses in his front overall's pocket, walked out the door, yelled to Maudie he'd be back after a spell, and was gone, disappearing up the dirt path towards Clyde's diggins at his peculiar, rapid, swinging gait, his aged gray eyes reading the trees and birds and animals like a book as he passed them in the clear, warm June weather.

Twice he puckered and blew a chortling whistle, one to a meadowlark and one to a bluejay, his white, four-day whisker growth undulating slightly, and he smiled when the birds stopped and turned their quizzical eyes towards him and then answered.

"Clyde," Abner bellowed when he reached the small clearing amid the pines. "Clyde, you home?"

"Back here, Abner."

Abner skirted the cabin to find Clyde waist deep in a hole, four feet by six feet.

Abner's eyes popped. "Lord a mercy, who died?"

Clyde grinned. "Ain't no grave. I'm putting in a root cellar. Got to get ready for the grain when she comes. Besides, I can put up a few nuts and berries and maybe some apples in here too, once she's finished."

Abner looked at the twelve small plots of ground farther out behind the cabin, marked by pegs and string, that were Clyde's experiment. One plot for each seed sample. Three plots were absolutely bare, no growth of any kind. Five had produced an excellent crop of Russian thistle, sunflowers, morning glory and some sand burrs. One had produced the beginnings of a grain crop that had been grazed off to ground level by gophers the first of the month, so Clyde had carried water all one day and poured it in the gopher holes to drown them out and then shoveled dirt in them until they were packed solid. The other three plots were trying to grow something, although neither Abner nor Clyde had ever seen any sprouts like them before.

Clyde jammed the shovel blade into the moist earth and climbed out of the hole, brushing the dirt from his hands and sleeves as he walked over to Abner. He noticed the package for the first time.

"What brings you out here today?"

"You don't store grain in no root cellar. She'll sprout down there. You got to store it in a grain elevator. I come out here to deliver this package to you."

"Then I guess I'll build a grain elevator." Clyde didn't have the slightest idea what a grain elevator was, but he didn't want to let on to Abner about his ignorance, so he said,   "After I finish my root cellar."   The fact he had undertaken the wrong project bothered him for just a minute or two. "What's in the package?"

"Don't know. Says it's for you. From the governor."

Clyde's head jerked up and his eyes focused intensely on Abner's. Then he relaxed and began to chuckle. "You're funnin' of course.   Must be a big sample of wheat from the university. Let's have a look."

Inside the cabin, Clyde laid the box on the plank table and for the first time read the address.   It was typed with a genuine typewriter on a label that you licked and stuck on the package, and on the top part of the label was the name and address of the governor of the state of Idaho, Cornelius Potts, and a round thing stamped in the corner with a lady wrapped in gauze and holding a rolled-up paper in her hand and on the sides were smaller figures of miners and trappers and the sun and the mountains and around it was writing that said it was the great seal of the state.

Clyde stood bolt upright and gazed at Abner in shock.   Finally he said, "I wonder what's inside."

"Ain't but one way to find out. Open her."

Carefully, reverently, Clyde removed the paper, then clipped the string holding the heavy cardboard box closed.   He felt his breathing constrict as he placed his hands on the sides and slowly lifted the box lid.

Inside was a large sealed envelope, on top of a jet black garment of some kind.   Clyde's eyes narrowed in disbelief as he set the envelope on the table and lifted the robe out, letting it fall full length as he held it up.   He looked for a full half minute, trying to understand what it was.

"By thunder, Abner, I think the governor is figgerin' to make me a priest,!" he said in a hoarse whisper, his face a study in terror.

"Might be. What's the letter say?"

With trembling fingers Clyde opened the envelope and sorted out the documents: a three-page letter, and another three-page document with the words Constitution of the State of Idaho across the top of the front page in large letters.   Clyde pulled up a plank bench and sat down at the table, Abner standing behind him, and while Clyde read the governor's letter, his finger sliding down each line, Abner put on his glasses and read it over his shoulder.

When he finished, Clyde pushed the letter away and sat with his elbows on the table and stared at the far wall.   Abner walked around the table and sat down, staring back at him.

Finally Clyde said, "I think I misread it. Read it to me, Abner." His face was white.

Ten minutes later Abner dropped the letter back on the table top and licked his dry lips and for a while the two men stared at each other, their minds unable to accept the plain words in the letter.

Finally Abner swallowed and said, "I can't quite get hold of her, Clyde. I can't hardly get the words to come out. You are going to be a judge? Mary Lou Hubbard? Corvis Lumley? A regular lawyer from Boise coming to put her in jail?"

He shook his head and picked up the letter again. "If I hadn't seen this here writing with my own two eyes, I wouldn't have believed her. I can't believe her yet, and I'm sittin' here reading her. Clyde, what are you going to do?"

"When can I get mail back out to the governor?"

"Oh, probably early July. Get there sometime before mid-August."

"If I borrow Injun Charlie's mule and ride to Leadore, how much time?"

"I'd say, earliest, July fifteenth."

"Then I better git a pencil and git a letter back to the Governor. I ain't going to be no judge, and I ain't going to do nothing about Mary Lou and Corvis Lumley. Corvis got just what he had coming, rowing across the river to do mischief like always. No sir, I ain't going to do no such thing as be a judge or do nothing about Mary Lou."

"Can't do that, Clyde. Says here Hugh Fitzgerald is already on his way here to be the lawyer. Now what do you suppose a man with a name like Hugh Fitzgerald is going to be like?"

Clyde leaned back in his chair and his eyes widened. Irish! Big, barrel-chested, sandy hair, fists like hams, drinks moonshine from a bucket, sings like a bird, loses his temper in a trice and breaks things up when he gets disappointed. After he arrives and has had a bucket of moonshine, and then finds out he has come clear across the state only to be told by Clyde the trial is off . . . Clyde felt the blood drain from his head and he thought for a minute he was going to faint.

Wild-eyed, Clyde whispered, "I'm leaving, Abner." He started to rise to begin packing what few things he would need to spend a long time away from the Settlement.

"Can't do that, Clyde. They'll come git you."

Clyde's mouth fell open. "What for? I ain't done nothing."

"This here letter says you are all ready appointed a genuine state of Idaho district judge, for the case of Mary Lou Hubbard and she's signed by the governor, Cornelius Potts. Now what do you suppose the state does to judges who neglect their official duties? I reckon they hang 'em just like for being a traitor to the flag!"

Clyde gasped. "No sir, that ain't fair. I didn't have no say. That ain't American. I didn't get no vote on this. That just ain't American."

His breathing quickened as he realized he could find no way out.

"Don't make no difference. You got no choice. You got to stand right there and do your duty!"

"I won't. If I go to jail, I won't."

Abner shook his head ruefully and spoke quietly. "I said hang, Clyde. Not jail. Hang."

"Abner, you wouldn't hang me."

"Not me, you consarned fool. The sheriff."

Clyde slumped forward, face buried in his folded arms on the table. Abner reached over to pat him affectionately, trying to comfort him. For a long time the two men sat thus, across the table from each other, Clyde in the depths of torment, Abner patiently waiting while he occasionally patted the back of his head.

Finally Abner rose. "Clyde, tell you what. Don't make up no decisions about this right now. Read this letter and this other paper a couple of times tonight and think on it. Come on to my place tomorrow morning and let's decide what to do."

What else was there? Clyde just nodded his head, too desolate to utter a word.

5

FROM THE DOOR OF THE PLACE,
Abner saw Clyde coming and he knew something was wrong. By
the set of Clyde's jaw, the frown on his face, and the sturdiness of
his stride, setting each step like it was planted forever, Abner concluded that Clyde had wrestled with himself all night and had made
up his mind, and whatever he had decided meant trouble. Abner
had dealt with Clyde most of his life, enough to know he was usually slow and methodical in his thinking, but when he finished, he
was usually right, and he was a bulldog. Abner walked out into the
early morning sunshine to meet him. Clyde slowed as they came
together.

"I got my mind made up," Clyde started, without so much as his
usually cheerful howdy. "Let's go set in the place while I tell you
what I decided."

Seated opposite each other over a plank set on two empty bar-
rels, Abner on a pickle keg and Clyde on a nail box, Clyde plowed
into it like he had to get it all said before one piece fell out of place
and the whole thing came tumbling down.

"First thing, I got to go find Mary Lou. I don't figure to be no
judge on this if I don't know what she did, so I got to go find out."

He closed his eyes and puckered his forehead while he forced himself to remember what came next.

"Next thing, the letter says I got to get me a clerk. He's the most important one in the courtroom. A clerk is the one who hands me things when I ask for them and does everything I tell him to do to make this trial. He don't ask no questions. He just does it. And he's respectful. As of right now, Abner, you're my clerk."

Abner leaped from the pickle keg. "ME! I . . you . . I aint going to be no clerk!"

"You're too late. I already clerked you. They do clerks that shirk their duties just like they do judges. They hang 'em."

Abner stood frozen in his tracks. Clyde waited until the white left Abner's face and his breathing started again.

"Next thing, I got to get me a courtroom. I figure the second floor of the place is it. That means I got to get it cleaned out some and get it ready. Chairs and tables and such. You got just a few days to get her done."

"Me? Why me?"

"Because that's what clerks do, - what I tell 'em."

"Now just hold on a dang minute," Abner suddenly said as his mind began to lose its numb feeling. "The second floor is got a lot of pack rats and such and I ain't going to turn into a rat chaser just because you got a hair up your nose and think . ."

Clyde raised his hand and looked fierce and silenced Abner in midsentence. "Bad clerks get hanged, Abner. Git rid of the rats. Set some baits. Shoot 'em. The second floor is going to be the courtroom."

"Hanged? Tarnation! You think you're going to hang me?"

Abner's face was bright red, making his white hair and five-day beard stubble all the more white, and his neck veins stood out.

"Not me. The sheriff. You forgot already?"

Abner flamed and mumbled but could not say a word. Clyde stared at him until he clamped his mouth shut and sat back down on the pickle keg.

"Next thing, according to the letter, I got to get me a reporter. That's someone who writes down what happens. I figure that is going to have to be Maudie, because she's the only one I know handy that can write."

Clyde continued to tick off his memorized plan.

"Next thing, the letter says I got to get me someone to speak up for Mary Lou, like a lawyer. I thought on that all night. The best I can think of is Injun Charlie."

In the past ten years, Abner had seen Injun Charlie more than anyone else in the Settlement, and he could count those visits on the fingers of one hand. He lived four miles out of town in a small blind canyon where he had built a hogan of mud and sticks. Abner couldn't remember the man saying more than ten or fifteen words in the thirty years he had known him. He had no idea of his age. Some said eighty, some said one hundred. Abner reckoned him about eighty-three. His face was wrinkled and marked from chicken pox, and his hands looked withered. But he walked straight up and his obsidian eyes never stopped working. His huge, curved nose dominated his entire being. He usually just looked impassive while he watched and listened and clamped a homemade corn cob pipe between his teeth. He never had tobacco in the pipe; just held it clamped. He braided his long black hair, but wore the clothing of a white man.

"Injun Charlie? He aint going to say anything in a trial. Just sit there and suck on his pipe and listen to it squeak when the air goes through."

"I wondered about that. But I don't think so. Old Injun Charlie ain't dumb. He must have a lot inside to say because dang little of it has ever come out. He sees a lot and he's thinking all the time. He'll get it done."

Clyde closed his eyes and with an index finger extended, started counting off the things he had discussed. When he caught up to where he was, he continued.

"Now next thing, I got to get me a jury. The letter don't say anything about that, but the other paper, the constitution, does. This time of year, that aint going to be easy, what with the mines being open after the winter, and planting and going after venison and fish for winter and all. But here's how I figure it. If I work out a list and take three or four days on Injun Charlie's mule and ride a big circle, I can probably find enough to get the job done. I can't figure nothing else."

Abner shook his head, unable to improve on the plan himself.

After his original shock at becoming a court clerk, he had begun to accept the whole idea, tentatively, but still felt exasperation at Clyde for having done it.

"Next thing, the letter said I had to keep good track of all expenses, and that worries me. What expenses?"

Abner stood for a moment and scratched his scraggly white stubble. "I don't rightly have no idea," he finally conceded. "I can't see nothing in this thing so far to spend money on. I just don't rightly know."

"Well, maybe we'll figure it out before we're finished. Anyway, that's what clerks do. Keep track of expenses."

Clyde kept his face straight forward but peeked at Abner out of the corner of his eyes. In the time Clyde could remember knowing Abner, Abner had never kept one record of any kind in his store. He had it all in his head, accurate to the penny or the pig or the chicken, or whatever he had bargained for, and never forgotten.

To Clyde's surprise, Abner hardly hesitated. "I'll keep your expenses record." Then Abner turned and finished his thought. "That way there won't be any."

Clyde didn't want to make a fuss about it right then, so he continued.

"In the constitution paper, I read one part that I can't figure out. It says everybody charged with a felony is entitled to a speedy trial. Now, what is a felony?"

Clyde raised his eyes to Abner's, hoping against hope he would know.

"That ain't hard. That is a serious crime. Like murder."

"Is attempted murder, like we got here, a felony?"

"I don't know. Murder is pretty bad, depending on who done it and why, but if you just take a crack at it and miss, well, maybe that ain't so bad. I don't know."

Clyde chewed the inside of his cheek as he reflected on it. "Well, I can't take no chance on it. I got to think it is a felony crime, which means I got to give Mary Lou a speedy trial."

He stood and looked Abner straight in the eyes. "Now what does it mean, a speedy trial?"

Abner, his small, wiry frame a full six inches shorter than Clyde's five feet ten inches, drew his face into a prune, so intense was his thought.

"I never heard of that before. I don't know what that means. Maybe it means you got to do the trial real quick after the crime. Makes sense that way, so the evidence is fresh and nobody has time to figure out how to lie about it."

"Maybe," said Clyde slowly. "I thought of that. But maybe it means that when you do the trial, you got to do it speedy. Get it done quick, so nobody has time to find a way to slip something crooked into it somewhere."

Abner shook his head as he began to pace. "Yeah, maybe that could be."

"Well, whichever it is, I figured out a way to take care of both notions. I'm going to set the trial for a week from tomorrow, which is as quick as I think I can find a jury and get Injun Charlie to speak for Mary Lou and get back here to do it. And I'm going to start her at nine o'clock that morning and finish her by noon. Now that ought to be speedy enough for just anybody who might want to ask, no matter which notion they got about a speedy trial."

He looked at Abner for confirmation, certain his plan would work.

"That just might do it. Nobody can complain about that."

"Only worry I have is that state lawyer. The letter said he left Boise a week ago. Just like one of those city boys to get lost out here. If he ain't got the sense to find his way here, then that's his fault. I'll just conduct the trial without him and he can straighten out his ignorance with the governor when he gets back. What do you think?"

"Well, he still has eight days. He ought to make it easy in that time."

"That's what I say. So I give him enough time and if he don't make it, I go right ahead."

Again Clyde closed his eyes and ran his index finger down his mental check list. He heaved a big sigh when he realized he had remembered all of it but one or two little details.

"One more thing. The letter says I got to make up a written judgment on this trial when it's finished so it's official. That's what reporters do. So I put you in charge of Maudie to get the judgment written up."

Clyde had thought long and hard to find a way to throw Abner a bone, make him feel important.

Abner thought for a moment and sort of liked being put in charge of someone else for a change.

"All right," he said. "I remember reading a book about a trial back several years. Maybe I still got it somewhere in the store. I'll find it while you're gone, and get some pointers."

"And finally, one last thing. I ain't going to wear that robe."

Abner hardly hesitated. "Yep, you are. I doubt the trial is legal unless you wear the robe." He grinned a vengeful, devilish grin of revenge.

"And they hang judges that don't do their sworn duty. Remember?"

Clyde swung around to face him squarely.

"Then you just write them a letter right now and tell them to send the sheriff with the rope. I'll make the trial and I'll do all them other things, but I will not wear that dumb robe. If they hang me for it, I won't wear it."

Abner had never expected such a reaction.

"Suit yourself. I'll have to think it over, whether I write the governor to ask about it or not. I'll just have to think that one over."

Abner wondered how he could use this new power to keep from becoming a rat chaser.

6

"BLACKMAIL! THAT'S WHAT ABNER done. Just plain blackmail."

In the crystal clear, dry mountain air, beneath an absolutely cloudless blue sky that seemed to reach forever, Clyde allowed a small smile to tug. Behind him, following a spectacular sunrise, the sun had just cleared the farthest ridge of purple mountains, giving full light to the layers upon layers of ridges and valleys that spread around him as far as his eyes could see. The deep purple of the near mountains lightened with each succeeding layer, all of them crowned and carpeted with the magnificent emerald green of pines and firs, with small streams running between the ridges to collect into larger ones, then finally into the mighty Snake River, winding its ancient course to the Pacific Ocean, sparkling in the sunlight to his right.

Around him birds sang everywhere, chipmunks scolded, a porcupine waddled down towards the trail, and six white tailed deer raised their delicate heads, huge eyes and ears motionless as they decided he was a friend and resumed grazing.

Beneath him, Injun Charlie's faithful old mule Buttercup plodded along, head rising and falling with each stride, on down the mountain trail leading to the home of Caleb and Clara Peabody. It was mornings like this that renewed Clyde's reasons for wanting to spend his life in these mountains.

"Just kept working at me about wearing that robe until I had to help him get the place ready for court or get in trouble."

Together, Abner and Clyde had swept the place out and set rat baits and then scrubbed the worst-smelling places with lye soap so strong it made the hot water bubble and boil and their hands burn when they got wet. Abner agreed to get the benches and tables while Clyde made his ride to round up a jury.

Before Clyde left the settlement, he had talked old Gibbons into being on the jury, if Homer would tend the livery and the grain store for him. That made one. In the five days since then, he had talked with Mary Lou to get the facts about the shooting, made her promise to be in the Settlement for the trial, persuaded Injun Charlie to speak for Mary Lou, borrowed his mule, and visited eleven other farms or cabins belonging to people he hoped to use on the jury. Three of them were not at home and could not be found. Four others just absolutely could not leave their summer work to do it.

So of the eleven, just four had agreed to come on in and be on the jury, and Gibbons made five.

The first was the pigtailed Chinese who wore a funny, flat, woven straw upside down hat and grew vegetables on half an acre on the river bottom and sold them to families up and down the river. Because he spoke only a few words of English, no one knew his name, so he was just called Lee.

He had listened intently while Clyde carefully explained the whole trial to him, then nodded his head vigorously and tried to sell Clyde some turnips. Clyde tried one more time and this time he threw in his kicker about the meal at Maudie's. Lee suddenly nodded his head again and gestured he would come to the Settlement on the trial day. Eat much ham. Pie. Clyde left knowing Lee would be there, but fearful he thought it was a holiday celebration with a lot of Maudie's food for free.

Next there was Luke Tumfister. The old hermit lived up on the north slope of Hornsby Mountain, where he nursed a huge hole in the mountainside that he called a mine, and he insisted he was just days from a mother lode gold strike. The fact he had been just days from the strike for the past eleven years never bothered him. He quickly agreed to come, because his left leg was in a homemade splint and he couldn't do much besides sit around anyway. A four-ton rock had broken his leg ten days ago, so he set it himself, splinted it, and was just getting a good case of cabin fever when Clyde showed up to break the monotony. He would ride his old donkey, the one that pulled his ore carts out of the mine, and be there on trial day.

Third, there was Amos Two Fingers, a half-breed Indian who poached deer and distilled white lightning moonshine and dodged the law for a living. He used to be just Amos until one day nine years ago when his still blew up and a piece of the copper tank whacked off all but two fingers on his left hand, which earned him the nickname, Two Fingers. When he heard all the facts about Mary Lou, he agreed to come because he knew old Lumley. Why, he made the worst bootleg whiskey on the river, and ought to be put out of business anyway. And a man who would make bad moonshine just couldn't be trusted.

Fourth, Nathan Jensen figured it was his patriotic duty to leave his wife and kids and homestead for two days to come sit on the jury. He didn't see how Mary Lou Hubbard could be thought of as an attempted murderess.

It hadn't been easy. Before the jurors promised to come, they had asked a hundred questions. Did she do it? Have you talked with her? Who is going to talk against her? Why hasn't someone shot old Lumley long before now? Land a mercy, why don't they give her a reward? Is Lumley going to be there? Who is going to be the judge?

Clyde told them everything Mary Lou had told him, and answered all the other questions the best he understood them. But he soon discovered the big secret was a promise of a free meal at Maudie's. Venison ham roast and mashed potatoes and peas and corn, with fresh-picked blueberries. Once you got them licking their lips, hit them with a piece of her apple pie and fresh milk. Of the five that had promised to come, Clyde knew at least three of them were coming for the meal, not the trial.

And that's the first of the expenses, he thought. I figger if the governor had meant to limit those expenses he would of said so. So he'll just have to pay for those meals at Maudie's.

The trail leveled into the valley and the mule sloshed across the shallow stream towards the log house where Clara Peabody was raising her brood. Sixteen years ago, when she was seventeen and married Caleb Peabody, Clara had been a tall woman with a big-boned frame, a large, round face that was so open and honest you never noticed it was homely, an unending joy in life, and a heart with enough love in it for every member of the human race.

Fifteen years ago she gave birth to her first child, a large, raw-boned boy, much like herself. Last February she gave birth to her fifteenth child, a girl, making nine boys and six girls so far, one each year. Caleb discovered ten years ago that in order to get the cash money to pay for some things they could not make with their own hands, he had to go work the mines, either north at Goldsboro or south at Leadore, for the summer months. Clara and the kids had to get in the necessary row crops of carrots, potatoes, turnips and cabbages for the root cellar, gather nuts and dry some berries and take care of the pigs and milk cow and calf for meat and shoot a couple of deer during those months.

With Clara swamping the children with love every day, the Peabody home was known as a sort of loving, muddled up, friendly place to be, where visiting youngsters would be swept up with the Peabody kids and fed, prayed over, scrubbed, and assigned daily chores just like all Clara's kids, mostly because she just loved kids and never stopped to sort them out. Any grownups who showed up got hugged by her, fed something, called darlin' and deary and sent on their way with her calling God bless you and waving until they were out of sight.

All this had affected her appearance. Whereas she was tall and square at seventeen, now, sixteen years and fifteen kids later, she was tall and shaped like a teepee. There were few interruptions between her shoulders and her ankles to alter the lines of her loose, nearly colorless dress. Her ample bosom, once remarkable, had long since abandoned beauty for the practicality of nursing fifteen children in fifteen years. Volume she still had; shape she didn't.

Byron Peabody, the oldest of the Peabody kids at fifteen and the largest at six feet three inches and two hundred twenty pounds, was the first to spot Clyde coming in. He bellowed a howdy and dropped the shovel he was using to shovel pig manure into a wheelbarrow to spread on the strawberries to make them sweeter. As though by magic, ten other round faces appeared from work stations all over the house and garden and the kids came running. Clyde lifted his right leg forward and slipped off Buttercup, catching the three heavy burlap bean sacks he had been using in place of a saddle.

"Howdy the house," Clyde responded as the front door swung open and out came Clara, holding the four-month-old baby to her bosom, which was unceremoniously exposed outside her unbuttoned dress while the baby took its breakfast.

"Well howdy yourself, darlin'. Come on in. Land a livin' it's good to see you Clyde. Byron, fetch some of them berries Lizzie picked yesterday and some fresh milk and come a-runnin'. We got a visitor."

Bradley and Billy, the fourteen-and thirteen-year-olds, took Buttercup's lead rope and tied her to the water trough, and then ran to join the throng that was all around Clyde as he walked up the front steps onto the planks of the front porch.

Clara tenderly tugged the tiny mouth from her bosom and drew in her stomach and expertly buttoned a couple of buttons on her dress to meet social requirements, and as Clyde walked onto the porch she stepped to him and hugged him soundly with her free arm, holding the baby to one side for a minute.

"Such a beautiful mornin' to have a caller. Come on in, dearie, and set a minute. Just passin' this way or is there somethin' I can do for you?"

Clyde would never have believed fifteen children could assemble in the kitchen and remain still enough to let him talk with Clara, but they did.

"Clara, I got a thing coming up day after tomorrow that I don't know what to do with."

Ten minutes later he leaned forward, hands clasped on the huge kitchen table, and studied Clara's eyes.

"So I couldn't think of no one else to finish making up the jury than you. I know what you got to do here, and I purely hate asking, but I don't see no other way."

Then he sprung his fetcher on her, hoping.

"You'll get a venison ham dinner at Maudie's. Free."

Clara's eyes became thoughtful. "Thanks, but the meal aint that important. Did Mary Lou do it? Is she guilty?"

"'Course not. She shot the holes in the boat all right, but she never hurt old Lumley, and she never meant to."

Clara started shaking her head, slowly at first. "And now that pretty little slip of a girl has got to go on trial for attempted murder on account of that old scoundrel Lumley. Land a livin', that ain't right. No sir, that ain't right."

Clare rose to her full height.

"Well," she asked Byron, "kin you handle things here for about a day and a half? You and Lizzie?"

Byron did not flinch. All he had known since he could remember was handling things here. Of course he could.

"Clyde, you got to understand, I'll have to bring little Gloria with me, and Bernie and Bennie too. They're just too small to leave here alone with Byron. And Becky will have to come to tend them while I'm in the place."

"That's all right. Just bring them on in."

"And I'll have to bring Buddy to drive the team. Byron, can you keep it afloat here with the rest?"

"We'll keep her afloat, Mama."

"Okay. Bless you, Byron. All of you. I'll be there, Clyde. Now you sit right there and eat them blueberries with that cream, hear?"

7

"IF THE SETTLEMENT ISN'T JUST OVER
this hill, I'm going to lie down under the nearest tree and die. Just
not get up. That couldn't be worse than this."

Hugh Fitzgerald was walking spraddle-legged, moving his body
with each step so his legs didn't rub together, and muttering to himself under his breath. Above his waist he wore only his shirt.
Below his waist he wore his shoes and socks. In between, he wore
nothing. The inner parts of his thighs, and between his legs, were
an eruption of raw, red hamburger. Perspiration brought on by the
heat of the early afternoon sun and the struggle of walking while
leading the old U-necked, spavined, ring-boned mule were causing
him to grit his teeth every time perspiration ran onto his lower
regions, and he was using his shirt to wipe it before it got that far.

His suit coat and vest and trousers, with his carpetbag and the
extra change of clothes, were jammed under the pack saddle ropes
on the mule.

When the road ran out three days ago, he bought the mule for
ten dollars to ride the last fifty eight miles of the journey to the
Settlement, but no one told him the saddle was a pack saddle. He
learned that from an old prospector two days later, whom he left sit-

ting on the ground wheezing in a laughter convulsion.

When the pack saddle had worn him raw between his legs, he took it off the mule and tried to ride bareback, but soon decided the razor-sharp spine of the old mule was worse than the pack saddle after it reduced his inner legs to a red hot fire of irritated, bleeding pulp. He strapped the saddle back on and resolved to walk the last forty five miles. The next day he laid his suit coat, vest, and change of clothes across the pack saddle to make it a little softer and tried it again and it partially worked, except the rubbing of his wool trousers against his raw legs soon inflamed them again. He tried walking again, only to discover that the damage was too heavy; there was no stopping it. The longer he walked the worse it got, until he took his woolen trousers and underwear off and walked with nothing on save his shirt and shoes and socks. He hadn't seen a soul for two days, so being without trousers or underwear held no fear for him.

As he approached the crest of a hill, he closed his eyes in a silent prayer for deliverance or death. He didn't care which. When he opened his eyes, he was looking down a slope at the Settlement, in the center of which was the place.

"God lives and He loves me," he said, and let the reins to the old mule drop as he started down the slope, moving his body with each step as before.

The first thing he saw moving as he came onto the dusty flat was a substantial woman in a full-length dress and apron. She walked out onto the battered planking of the back sidewalk of a ramshackle, shot up, dilapidated, ancient building that dominated the clearing. She stopped, staring at him. Even at one hundred yards he could see the surprise and puzzle on her plain face.

Licking parched lips, he turned around, hoping against hope the old mule had followed him. It bumped into him as he turned, and then stopped, waiting for his next move.

"Thank you God," he said hoarsely to himself and drew the coat and vest and trousers from the pack saddle. He dropped the coat and vest in the dust, forgotten, and with his eyes batted against the pain, slowly slid one leg, then the other, into the trousers. He refused to button them shut; he could not stand the pain of wool on raw flesh. He just grabbed the front in both hands and let them hang as loose as he dared, and again began his crablike, slow pacing towards the woman.

He continued up to the edge of the porch where the woman waited. He saw in her eyes that she understood the whole thing long before he got there, but he didn't care. Facing her, he drew to his full height and said with as casual an air as he could muster, "Would there be a hotel nearby?"

"Sonny," the woman said with concern, "forget a hotel. You just better let me help you on in here."

Maudie stepped off the porch and reached an arm around his waist and all but lifted him onto the porch and inside.

"Now you just lay right down there on that bed and let me get some water and we'll see what we can do about this."

Hugh sacrificed pride for practicality. He lay down on the bed as ordered, keeping his legs spread wide apart, and watched while Maudie got a huge wooden wash tub off in a corner at the rear of the large storeroom and filled it with water, some of it hot. She tested it with her elbow, then strung a sheet on a line to give him privacy and turned to him.

"Now take this soap and go get into that tub. It's cool but even so it's going to smart some when you first sit down. Wash real good between your legs. Now git at it."

The water stung at first, and he thought he was on fire when he started with the soap, but he finished and dried and reached for his underwear and trousers.

Maudie called, "Finished with the bath? Fresh change of soft cotton drawers right behind you on the peg. But don't put 'em on yet."

"Finished," he said.

"Okay. Wrap that towel around you and get back on out here and lay on your tummy. We got some doctorin' to do."

He wrapped the towel and grabbed the soft cotton underwear and walked back to the bed, a little less stiff-legged.

"Lay down right there," she directed.

Watching her like a hawk, he lay down.

In one stroke Maudie pulled the towel away and separated his legs. Hugh jerked rigid and started to roll over. "Just what do you think you're doing?" he cried. "Give me that towel!"

"Forget the towel and flop back down there, son. You get any funny ideas, I'll drop you in your tracks. You got a pretty fair start on infection up there between your legs, and judging where it is and the direction it's spreading, you best lay quiet or you can just forget about having any kids. If you're worried about me seeing you naked, doctorin' just about everybody around here I seen more bare bottoms than you seen dressed, so it don't mean nothing to me. I'm going to step over there and get some salve. You lay still.!"

Chagrined, embarrassed, red-faced, Hugh started to turn to grab again for the towel, realized he still wore no clothes, and rolled back onto his stomach to preserve what modesty he could. Maudie shook a stern finger as she quickly walked to a cupboard and returned.

She opened a large, round, flat can of brown, sharp salve, scooped out a generous load on four fingers, spread his legs farther, and started working it into everything above his knees that was red. Hugh jerked to protest and Maudie shoved his head back down and kept rubbing.

The fire subsided and Maudie said, "There. That ought to do it. Feel some better?"

"Thank you," Hugh said stiffly.

Maudie grinned. "Now you stay right there for a while. When did you eat last?"

Hugh mumbled, "Yesterday maybe. I don't remember. I'm not hungry."

"I'll rustle around here and get something for you."

Ten minutes later she plopped a large bowl of hot venison and vegetable stew with a large slice of home-baked bread in front of him.

"There's some dinner. I'll go see what happened to your mule. Be right back."

Five minutes later she returned to find the bowl empty and wiped clean by the bread.

"Thank you," Hugh said quietly, a little less chagrin in his voice.

"Here." Maudie spread a sheet over him. "With the salve on, we can give you back some privacy. After all this, I reckon I ought to know who you are, son."

"I am Hugh Fitzgerald."

Maudie went into hysterics. Hugh looked at her, then past her, then behind himself, probing for whatever had caused it. When she quieted enough to talk, Hugh smiled a sarcastic smile and asked, "That name is pretty funny?"

"Name's fine. It was me. Are you the man sent in here to do the trial against Mary Lou Hubbard?"

"Yes I am."

"It's just that we expected some great big lubber of an Irishman. And we got you."

"I'm Irish," he said with an edge in his voice. He had labored his entire life with the knowledge that his physical appearance just didn't meet people's expectations of an Irishman. Suddenly his eyes sharpened as he realized Maudie knew about the trial.

"Would you please tell me what place this is and who you are and how you knew about the trial?"

"You're in the Settlement and I'm Maudie."

Hugh jerked bolt upright. "The Settlement? This is the Settlement?"

"You found us."

"The Mary Lou Hubbard Settlement?"

"The same." Maudie was grinning.

His mouth agape, his eyes wide, Hugh looked around the comfortable clutter of Maudie's establishment, then out the door into the bright sunlight at the dust and finally the trees.

"Where's the courthouse? Where's the judge?"

"Courthouse is upstairs. The judge is out rounding up a jury."

"Rounding up a jury? Is the trial date already set?"

"Yep. Day after tomorrow. Nine o'clock sharp."

Hugh tried to leap from the bed but with the stiffness and the rash his leap came closer to a mild twitch. He groaned, then nearly shouted, "Impossible! Day after tomorrow? What kind of a court is this? Where's Corvis Lumley? I must talk with Corvis Lumley. Get me my clothes. Where's the jail? Where's the defendant? I've got to get out of here. Which direction to the Lumley home?"

Maudie, who outweighed him sixty pounds easily, put both hands on his shoulders and pinned him back down.

"You aint going nowhere until morning, earliest. If you intend making that trial you just settle down and things will work out fine. There ain't no jail. Mary Lou is at home. I can point you toward Lumley's tomorrow."

8

"ABNER, THAT YOU UP THERE moving around?" Clyde batted at his trouser legs and shirt sleeves to get the trail dust out as he wearily climbed the stairs from Abner's store to the second floor of the old building. "That you making the racket?" The glow of the setting sun came through the west bank of windows in golden shafts.

"No, that ain't me," came the answer. "It's them two big pack rats that eats our baits like they was candy and comes looking for more. Of course it's me. You're back. Did you get her done?"

Clyde stepped into the big, bare room and for a moment gave it a critical inspection.

"I got her done. Mary Lou'll be here in the morning, and six people are coming for the jury. Injun Charlie will talk for Mary Lou."

He paused because the next question was important.

"Did Hugh Fitzgerald get here?"

Abner went into gales of laughter. "He got here. A little bitty boy. Left at daybreak this morning to go get Lumley for the trial. Walking peggity-legged and all spraddled out."

Clyde stopped and looked at him, waiting for an explanation.

"He's from the city of Boston," Abner explained. "Rode a pack saddle for two days not knowing it wasn't a regular saddle. Maudie fixed up his behind, but he's sure going to be stiff-legged a day or two. Aint seen him since dawn, but I reckon he'll be here come nine o'clock in the morning."

"A boy?" Clyde asked, standing stock still.

"A little teeny golden-haired, blue-eyed boy! Graduated from one of them big name eastern colleges a month ago and come directly here to learn about the world. Never seen anything west of Boston 'til this month." Abner shook his head with a wry smile. "Pecky little bugger though. Just pegged it right on down to the river and rowed a boat over to Lumley's. At least that's the direction he was going when we last saw him. He's never rowed a boat before, but he just took right holt and started out. If he didn't learn to allow for the current, he's likely passing Leadore about right now."

"Well, if he's here, it looks like we got us a trial. You ready?"

"I think so." With considerable pride showing, Abner explained, "That table right there is where you and me sit. That's so we can whisper answers back and forth on hard problems. We sit on them two chairs." The table and chairs were along the north wall of the room.

Abner walked over to the long, rough cut plank bench that stood at right angles to the table, in front of the east wall. "Here is where the jury sits. If they sit real quiet, I don't figger they'll get any slivers."

He pointed to a smaller table opposite the jury bench, in front of the west wall. "That's where Maudie sits to keep her papers." Then he pointed to the last large table, beside the smaller one, also opposite the jury bench. "And that's where Hugh Fitzgerald and Lumley sits, along with Injun Charlie and Mary Lou."

"Think that's safe, what with old Lumley sometimes getting real excited and all?"

"I thought of that. So I painted this here line down the middle of the table, and you'll just have to tell old Lumley that if he crosses that line, you'll contempt him." Abner's chin rose an extra inch or two as he sprung the word "contempt" on Clyde.

"Contempt? How do I contempt him?"

"That means you make him pay five dollars." Abner's eyes began to glow with pride. "While you was gone I dug up that old book about a trial and I learned some good words. A lot of them. So you just tell Lumley you'll contempt him if he crosses that line."

"What about where the witnesses sit while they're telling the jury their story?"

Abner's face fell. " I . . . well, I forgot about that. We'll just get a chair or a milking stool and put it smack in the middle of this whole thing, facing us. That way everybody can see and hear the witness."

""Well, I hope that is all we need. Did this little kid have anything to say about the trial? Any suggestions?"

"Well, yes and no. I don't know how to read him. Yesterday evening when I told him you was out getting the facts from Mary Lou and rounding up a jury, he went real quiet for a few minutes but didn't say much. Just sort of puffed up and looked red for a minute, then started looking normal again."

"Think he got mad about something?"

"I wondered. But I don't think so. When I told him we were going to crank up the trial at nine o'clock and have her finished by noon, he went white, not red, and just sort of looked glassy-eyed for a minute and walked away and stood over there looking out the windows."

Clyde puckered his face in thought as Abner continued.

"So I don't know if red or white is his mad color. Whichever, he just all of a sudden walked back on down to Maudie's and got ready to leave this morning and he's been gone since daylight."

"Well," Clyde said slowly, "we'll just have to worry about that come morning. I got to get home and see what shape my diggins are in after being gone so long. I better get walking. I'll see you in the morning."

"Hold on, Clyde. Set right down here. I got some words you got to know if you're going to get through this trial. I got them from that book, and you need to sleep on them, so sit down."

Reluctantly Clyde walked to the table and sat down in his chair while Abner sat down in his own.

"Now, you all ready know 'contempt.' So the next word you got

to know is 'prosecutor'. He's Hugh Fitzgerald. He's the one that
has to say Mary Lou looks guilty. Prosecutor. Got that? Okay.
Remember, he gets to put on his witnesses first. Then, the one that
says all the good things about Mary Lou is the defense counsel.
That's Injun Charlie. Got that? He puts on his witnesses when the
prosecutor is done. Got that? Okay? Defense counsel."

Abner shifted in his chair and his eyes were glowing again with
pride.

"Then there's 'objection'. When the prosecutor says something
defense counsel don't like, defense counsel can say 'objection.'
Okay? When one of them says that about the other one, then you
got to make a ruling. If you think one of them shouldn't of said
what he said, then you say 'sustained.' 'Sustained' means you think
he shouldn't of said it either. But if you like what he said, then you
say 'overruled.' Okay? Got that? Sustained, I didn't like it either.
Overruled, I did like it. Got that?"

Clyde nodded and began cleaning the fingernails on his right
hand with the index fingernail on his left.

"Now, the next one, you got to learn when to say 'admitted.'
That means if one of them wants to get something out in front of
the jury like a piece of paper or maybe a bullet, they say, I want this
admitted, and you say, 'admitted.' Then I admit it and its evidence
just like the words that are spoke. Okay? Get that?   Admitted,
which means it is evidence."

Abner closed his eyes to concentrate on what he wanted to say
next, and continued.

"The next one you already know. People who say something in
a trial are the witnesses. Why I'm telling you about witnesses is
because you got to remember to have me swear at them because it
ain't official if I don't. You just tell me to do it and I swear at them.
I got it memorized so don't worry about it. And after I swear at
them then you tell them to sit on the chair out there in the middle
and you call it the witness chair. Can you remember that?"

Clyde nodded as he slipped the index finger nail on his left hand
under the fingernail of his fourth finger on his right hand to clean it.

"Now, next is 'order in the court.' If anyone gets to raising a
ruckus about anything you just whack the table a good one and
holler 'order in the court.' Then they stop. If they don't, you con-

tempt them."

"With my fist? I whack the table with my fist?"

Abner looked at Clyde with a red face. "I never thought of that. That don't make sense. I'll get my hammer. Whack her a good one with that."

"Might split the planks." Clyde ran a hand over the rough cut planks.

"Then I'll wrap some burlap around her so she won't hit so hard."

"Okay," Clyde said. "I'll whack her with that."

"Then there's what the jury finally decides about Mary Lou. That's called the verdict. A latin word." Abner paused to let Clyde get hold of the fact he knew a Latin word. "So when the trial is over you turn to the jury and you say, 'what's your verdict?' And they say 'guilty' or they say 'not guilty'. There ain't no third verdict. Just one or the other."

Clyde gave up cleaning his finger nails and began shaking his head. "Abner, how am I supposed to get all that straight before morning?"

"It ain't hard, Clyde. Here. I'll walk a spell with you on your way home. I'll run her all past you again, and then you be here in the morning early and I'll run her past you again. Maybe I'll think of some more by then."

Reluctantly Clyde walked over to the staircase in the northwest corner of the dusky room and started down, Abner right behind him, still talking.

"Now, one more thing. I don't think she's going to be a legal trial unless you wear that black robe, Clyde."

Clyde stopped on the staircase and turned, his jaw set.

Abner continued. "And it appears you ain't going to wear it, so to keep this thing as legal as I can, I figure I'll have to wear the robe. Otherwise I think the governor will just declare this whole thing illegal and we'll have to do her over again."

Clyde continued on down the stairs, through the store and out into the sunset.

Abner asked, "Tell me who you got for the jury. I know about Gibbons, but who else is coming in?"

9

AT 8:45 A.M. ABNER SAT HIS OLD, battered wind-up alarm clock with the bell on top in the center of the table where he and Clyde were to sit. The glass front was long since broken and gone. The minute hand was bent so the arrow point showed two minutes more than it should and the hour hand had lost its point thirty years ago. The wind up key on the back was wound tight and the alarm was set for noon.

Clyde was impatiently pacing in the courtroom, mumbling over and over to himself, sustained, overruled, prosecutor, defense counsel, contempt, admitted, order in the court, verdict, and pausing between each to recite to himself what each meant.

Suddenly Abner straightened and cocked an ear, then walked to the row of open windows on the east side of the room, gazing out to the east of the building into the peace of a still, beautiful June morning. He quickly located the source of the loud, profane commands of a mule-skinner that he had heard faintly at first, then growing louder, and when he recognized who and what was coming, his head jerked forward, his frizzled old Adam's apple bobbing up and down with excitement.

"Clyde, come a-running. Take a look yonder!"

In a moment Clyde was beside him, head thrust forward, eyes wide in disbelief. Coming across the clearing was a team of mules, driven by someone neither man knew. Hooked to the mules was a huge skid, and on the skid was Corvis Lumley's rowboat!

Walking defiantly beside the rowboat, Corvis held his head high and his chest thrown out, his silent declaration that he finally had the goods on the Hubbards and he sure was not going to miss his chance.

On the other side, walking on legs held stiff and wide apart, was Hugh Fitzgerald. His chin was high, his jaw set firmly, his handsome, boyish face set in a scowl that was as close as he could come to looking like one charged with carrying The Sword of Justice.

The makeshift skid proceeded right up to the east side of the building, where the mule-skinner hollered, "Whoa there, you long-eared heathens, WHOA before I take yer hides!" When they stopped, the man quickly unhooked the tugs and traces from the singletrees and moved the mules a few paces ahead, then went back to Lumley and collected his jug of moonshine and moved off back across the clearing towards the river, driving his mules. Lumley and Hugh started towards the front of the place.

At that moment Abner turned an ear towards the west bank of open windows and quickly walked across the big second-floor room, again quickly locating the source of sounds of an incoming wagon.

"Well, here comes Clara Peabody and a passel of her kids, and I can see Luke Tumfister coming on his old donkey, and Amos Two Fingers not far behind. Looks like things are starting to pop right along."

Clyde didn't look up from his deep concentration as he paced, mumbling order in the court, verdict, contempt . . .

Hugh stopped in Maudie's only long enough to change from his work clothes to his suit, which Maudie had cleaned and pressed, and then he and Lumley marched up the stairs to the second floor.

"Where is the prosecutor's table," Hugh asked matter-of-factly.

"Right here," Clyde said, pointing. "You get this half and the other side gets the other half, past this line. Now I got to tell you, if you or Lumley gets past that line, I got to contempt you. You understand that?"

Hugh looked at the line, puzzled, then shrugged his shoulders and signaled to Lumley to come sit down. Hugh was standing with his feet close to a yard apart and after Lumley sat down, he gingerly straddled the bench and sat down with great care, a grateful smile forming as he eased onto his backside. He turned his head to Lumley and began his last-minute instructions.

Next, Lee appeared at the top of the stairs with Luke Tumfister right behind. Abner quickly walked towards them and said, "Right over here. This here bench is for the jury."

Hugh's head jerked up and he turned to look at the first of the jurors. His mouth dropped open and his eyes bugged as Lee shuffled over to the bench with his quick, small, peculiar steps, his pigtail swaying behind. Luke stumped on over to the bench using his good leg and a homemade crutch to protect his broken one. He was wearing exactly what he had been wearing for the last month. Battered bib overalls, an old blue woolen shirt, beat-up brogan shoes, and his ragged black felt hat, which showed dust and weather stain accumulated over twenty years. His four-year beard showed tobacco stains and a fair smattering of his menu for the past several days. The splint was on the outside of the overalls, and the two boards were extended beneath the level of his foot, so it went thump each time he took a step.

Amos Two Fingers quietly slipped into the room nearly undetected, an art he had developed in his moonshine business because he had soon found it was often convenient to come and go without anyone knowing. He was wearing a pair of whipcord pants, a dirty white shirt closed at the throat but with no tie, and broad, black suspenders, and his long black hair was pulled back and tied behind his head with a leather string. His black eyes never stopped moving, taking in at once everyone and everything in the room.

"Buddy," Clara's voice came drifting up the stairwell, "now you stay right here with Becky, and you keep them kids under control. Play with them a spell. If Benny has to wee-wee, you take him right on over to the outhouse and help him." Clara was clomping up the stairs as she gave the orders over her shoulder to the four she was leaving behind. Held tightly to her bosom was little Gloria, or Glory as she was called.

She heaved herself up the last step into the room and stood a moment, puffing. "Land a mercy, that was a climb. Howdy, everybody. Clyde, I need to sit. Where does the jury sit? And I don't reckon anyone here will take offense if I got to nurse Glory soon. 'Course not. Where's Mary Lou? Who's this nice looking young man? Am I late?"

Abner helped her to the bench and she heaved herself onto it in a lump and immediately laid Glory on her lap, opened her blanket, and stuck a finger into her diaper. "Done it again." She reached inside a paper bag she had under one arm and pulled out a fresh diaper, took of the messed one, wiped Glory's bottom without so much as a glance around, and put the fresh one on, closing the huge diaper pin in front.

"There," she beamed. "Now that feels good, don't it, little darlin." She wrapped the baby again and laid her against her shoulder. She stuffed the messed diaper into the bag with the fresh ones.

Hugh moved for the first time since Lee had appeared at the top of the stairs. He closed his mouth long enough to lick his lips, then let it fall back open again, his eyes still bugging.

Abner looked at the clock. "This here court is due to start in three minutes. I'll fetch Maudie. Anybody seen Gibbons or Nathan Jensen?"

Amos Two Fingers said quietly, "Nathan will be along directly. One of his kids fell down the well just as he was leaving. Had to fish him out. Told me to tell you. Said to go ahead and start without him."

Abner hollered down the stairwell, "Maudie, you hear me?" He cocked his head and waited, but there was no reply. "I'll have to get her."

Two minutes later they clambered up the stairs and Maudie took her place at the table. Gibbons came behind her and took his place on the jury bench.

Abner looked around the room and realized Mary Lou and Injun Charlie were not there. He looked at Clyde and shrugged. "I got one more official act I got to do and then we'll start. If Mary Lou don't get here on time we'll just go ahead without her." He moved quickly to the stairs and his shoes clumped as he rapidly walked down.

A minute later Hugh jerked his head to break the spell that had

possessed him for several minutes and began to protest about starting the trial without the defendant being present, but he was too
late. Abner was all ready coming back up the stairs, his steps slow-
er and at an even cadence.

When he emerged at the top of the stairs the courtroom became
silent as a tomb. His face was set, eyes straight ahead, his expression one of weighty authority. The black robe, large enough for a
man Clyde's size, hung on him like a tent, with two feet of it drag-
ging behind. One of his gnarled old hands held up the front to keep
him from tripping. He walked directly to the chair he was to occu-
py and stood, surveying everyone in the courtroom in sober dignity.

Luke Tumfister sniggered out loud through his scraggly beard
and Lee clapped his hand over his mouth. Maudie lolled back and
shook in silent laughter. Abner ignored them.

"Land a mercy, Abner, if that don't make it all official!" Clara's
voice broke the silence as she looked at him admiringly and Abner
smiled at her.

He cleared his throat and again the courtroom fell silent.

"This here trial is beginning. I'm the clerk and Maudie is the
reporter. Clyde is the judge. Over there is the jury. You all know
Corvis Lumley, and this here young man is Hugh Fitzgerald. He is
the prosecutor." When he used the word prosecutor, he glowed.

"Clyde, you better sit down here now."

He waited until Clyde sat down. "Mary Lou and Injun Charlie
aint got here yet and we still lack Nathan Jensen but we know why
he's late. We'll go ahead anyway. Clyde, you . . ."

They all heard the rustle on the steps. All eyes turned as Injun
Charlie's head appeared, and behind him came Mary Lou.

Hugh's eyes opened wider than they had ever opened before and
every muscle in his body locked. Mary Lou had carefully curled
and brushed her hair and it formed a halo around her face, then
hung halfway down her back in long, soft waves. Holding it was a
bit of yellow ribbon, tied with the bow on top. Her best dress of
white cotton with sky-blue checks was held in the middle by a
small belt covered with yellow cloth, accenting her flawless figure.
The toes of her mother's high-heeled button-up shoes showed under
the wide ruffle at the bottom of her dress.

A shaft of bright golden morning sunlight flooding through the east bank of windows bathed her in celestial glory. She looked around the room with her large, blue-violet eyes, smiling slightly and nodding silently to each person there in turn, each of whom she knew, until at last she came to Hugh.

When their eyes met, she froze. He was wearing his suit that Maudie had cleaned and pressed, with his high collar and black tie. He had brushed his blond curls well and his blue eyes glistened.

"Mary Lou, if you will just sit right over there with Injun Charlie, we'll start this trial."

Neither Mary Lou nor Hugh moved a muscle. They were lost in each other's eyes.

Abner looked at Clyde and Clyde shrugged and finally Abner cleared his throat loudly and said, "Injun Charlie, will you just take Mary Lou right over there with you and sit down?"

Injun Charlie gave one nod of his head and gently took Mary Lou's hand and sat her down. She was at one end of the bench and Hugh at the other, prosecutor and defense counsel between. Injun Charlie sat with his pipe clenched between his teeth and squeaked some air through it. Hugh looked at his wrinkled, ageless face and black braids and smelled the campfires and moved a few inches away. Injun Charlie squeaked some more air.

"All right. As I started to say, Clyde, you're the judge. Why don't you go ahead from here." Abner sat down beside Clyde and untangled his robe and turned towards him, waiting.

Clyde pulled his panic under control and started.

"This is the trial of Mary Lou Hubbard. You all know what she is charged with. Prosecutor Fitzgerald, if you want to put on any evidence, you can do that now."

Clyde sat back a little, the beginnings of hope springing in his chest at having gotten the trial under way.

Hugh rose, feet spread apart because of the rash. "Your honor, may I make some inquiries of the court?"

Clyde's eyes went blank. Quickly he ducked his head and turned to Abner and whispered, "Is he talking to me? I'm not no honor, I'm the judge, and when he's talking to the court, what does he mean? Who answers?"

Pain crossed Abner's face and he shot back, "Dang it Clyde, I forgot that one. They call the judge 'your honor'. You're your honor. When he says that, it's you. And when he talks to the court, that's you too. Answer him."

Clyde straightened, his eyes glazed. "What do you want to know?"

"Is this the defendant? This young lady?"

"Yes."

"Is she a juvenile?"

"I think she's a Methodist, if that means anything to you."

Hugh's eyes flickered for just a moment. "No, I mean, is she above twenty years of age?"

"No, she ain't."

"How old is she?"

"Seventeen, last I heard. Mary Lou, how old are you?"

"Seventeen. Eighteen come August twelfth."

"Then, your honor, this entire case ought to be conducted in a juvenile court, not a district court."

Clyde labored for a moment. "I don't know about that. I know the governor ordained me to do this and I'm going to do it. Now we only got until noon so we better get going. Do you want to have anybody witness?"

"Beg your pardon, your honor, are you going to try this girl as an adult?"

"She's a full seventeen, coming eighteen in two months. If you didn't see she's a full-grown woman when she walked over and sat down, then you got to be dead, Mr. Prosecutor Fitzgerald. Now, do you want someone to witness?"

"Does the defendant waive her rights and agree to be tried as an adult?"

Clyde ducked his head and whispered to Abner, "What's this waving thing?"

"Beats me," Abner whispered back, fear in his voice.

Clyde licked his lips and straightened. "I am going to go ahead with this trial. Mary Lou will do what she needs to do when Injun Charlie defense counsels her. Now let's get this thing going."

"Very well, your honor; may I spend a few minutes in a voir dire examination of the jury?"

Clyde froze and his eyes developed a one-thousand-yard stare for just a moment. He ducked his head towards Abner again. "What is a voir dire examination? For crying out loud, what for? They all look healthy to me."

"I don't know. He says that again, contempt him."

Clyde turned back and looked at Hugh. "I think they're all healthy enough to get through this trial. Ain't no place here private enough for an examination anyhow. I'm going ahead and if you don't . . . "

"Pardon me, your honor. All I want to do is ask the jurors a few questions to see if they are qualified to sit on this case."

"I already done that when I picked them to be on this jury. They are qualified. They know all about it, matter of fact."

Hugh's eyes began to show just a hint of panic. "You told these jurors about this case?"

"How can they decide if they want to be on the jury if they don't know about the case?"

Hugh paused in an obvious desperate attempt to grasp the picture that was rapidly developing.

Clyde seized the opportunity. "Now Mr. Fitzgerald Prosecutor, we already used ten minutes and we haven't done nothing about this trial. If you want someone to witness against Mary Lou, you better get them right there on the witness chair and get started. Otherwise I'm going to contempt you."

Not knowing what to expect from Hugh when he threatened him with contempt, Clyde grasped the handle of the hammer, ready to whack her on the table and call for order in the court if Hugh got huffy.

Hugh's head settled forward an inch and he looked at the hammer Clyde was fingering, with the head wrapped tightly in burlap and tied with a leather cord.

"May I ask what that is, your honor?"

"That is what I use for order in the court."

Hugh looked for the block that ordinarily attends a gavel, and there was none. He pursed his mouth for a moment as he considered just how Clyde used a hammer with the head wrapped in burlap to maintain order in such a courtroom. Another quick look at the jury and his worst suspicions seemed confirmed.

"All right now," Clyde said firmly, "one last chance. Do you want anybody to witness?"

Hugh hooked his thumb in the watch pocket of his vest and said, "The prosecution calls Corvis Lumley to the witness stand."

10

"WOULD YOU PLEASE STATE YOUR name," Hugh said in a clear, commanding voice.

Lumley, who had been sworn at by Abner, said, "Corvis Lumley."

"What is your residence?"

"I live in the state of Montana, just across the Snake River from here."

"For how long have you lived there?"

"All my life."

Hugh began to move on his feet, legs spread, waddling. "What is the nature of your work?"

"I am a farmer and I do a little gold prospecting too."

There was a general snigger and murmur among the jurors, who knew Lumley was a notorious moonshiner and bootlegger. Hugh ignored the interruption.

"Over the years have you become acquainted with a gentleman named Hubbard?"

"Yes I have."

"What is the nature of that acquaintance?"

"He's a dirty rotten skunk. That's the nature of the acquaintance."

Buzzing began in the courtroom and Clyde grabbed the hammer handle in case he had to whack her down to keep order in the court but the buzzing subsided and he eased it back onto the table.

Hugh glanced at Injun Charlie, expecting an objection, but with his eyes straight ahead, Charlie just squeaked his pipe.

"On what basis do you say he is a scoundrel, sir?"

"He salted my whiskey and he moulted my hens with a coyote so they wouldn't lay eggs for a month, that's why, and a lot of other things too."

"You sure this is the same Hubbard?"

"The same Clarence Hubbard."

"On Tuesday morning, just over two weeks ago today, did you have occasion to visit the residence of said Clarence Hubbard?"

"Yes sir I did."

"What was the occasion?"

"I figgered it was time we all forgot all the old dirty rotten things he done to me and I rowed across the river that morning to tell him so and offer to make friends and maybe we could do a little business together."

Luke Tumfister snorted and turned to Amos Two Fingers and whispered so loudly everyone heard, "Why don't he tell us about the rotten things he done to Clarence to start this whole thing to begin with, huh? Why don't he talk about that?"

Lumley partially raised from his witness chair and started towards the two men when he caught his temper and settled back down.

There was a general, loudly whispered concensus among the jury that Lumley ought to be made to tell about that, and exaggerated head nodding while Hugh waited and looked at them.

Then Hugh turned to Clyde. "Your honor, may I ask the court to direct the jury to remain silent and not discuss this case until all the evidence is in?"

Clyde worked that through his head and then said, "You people on the jury, don't make no more remarks out loud like that or I'll contempt you. If you want to ask Lumley questions, wait until Mr. Prosecutor Fitzgerald is finished. You'll all get your turn. Now let's get going. We used up forty minutes already."

Hugh's mouth dropped open and he said, "Your honor, is the court going to allow the jury to question the witnesses?"

Clyde looked vexed and Abner grabbed his arm and jerked him over and whispered, "The jury don't ask the questions, you dummy, the prosecutor and defense counsel do that."

Clyde's eyebrows arched and he whispered back sarcastically, "Nice of you to finally mention it." He turned back to Hugh. "No. What I meant was, if they got any doubts of what kind of a guy Lumley is, they get their turn after the trial is over. They can talk about that then. Let's move this thing along now."

Hugh bobbed his head in approval and continued with Lumley. "In short, sir, you were on a mission of friendship that beautiful summer morning?"

"That's what it was. Yes sir. A mission of friendship." Lumley nodded his head vigorously.

Hugh walked towards the end of the table, legs still spread. "How long did it take to row across the river?"

Before Lumley could answer, Clara scrooched her face and looked pained as she whispered to Gibbons, "Why is that poor boy walking like that? Why, he's hurtin' something awful."

Gibbons tittered, "Got galded riding a pack saddle and walking with wool pants. Maudie fixed him up. She told me." The entire jury panel heard it and erupted into gales of laughter.

Hugh jerked back towards them and his face reddened. He knew they had whispered but had no idea what about. "Your honor," he said, "could you instruct the jury . . ." He paused and shook his head sadly. "No, never mind. Strike that remark."

Clyde came alive. "Strike what? Who is striking who?" Clyde looked genuinely concerned something was going to happen and reached for the hammer handle to contempt the first one who made a move that looked like it could be striking someone.

"Nothing, your honor. Forget I said anything. May I continue questioning Mr. Lumley?"

"Yes, go ahead." Clyde eased the hammer back down.

"How long did it take you to cross the river, Mr. Lumley?"

"Oh, about twenty minutes or so, like always."

"Did anyone come with you?"

"No. I was alone."

"Describe the weather."

"Clear and dry. No clouds. Warm."

"Was the river calm?"

"Nice and calm."

"As you approached the Hubbard property, which way was your boat facing?"

"Well, it was facing nose in towards their boat landing."

"Where were you sitting in the boat?"

"On the plank in the middle like always."

"Which way were you facing?"

"The back of the boat. You got to sit that way to row."

"Did you keep the boat in the same position as you came to the landing?"

"No. As I come in to their landing I turned her around so I could see the house and the yard."

"Why was that?"

"I was worried old Hubbard might pull off another dirty trick and I wanted to see him first."

"So what happened then?"

"Well sir, as I was about twenty feet from the landing, I heard this whack right between my feet and then I heard a singing and a big bang and there was a bullet hole in the bottom of the boat. Right there between my feet!"

"What did you do?"

"Nothing. I just sat there. Then right on top of it there was five more whacks and sings and bangs and five more bullet holes and they was all leaking water into the boat real fast."

"Did you see who did the shooting?"

"Yes sir. Real quick I looked up there and Mary Lou Hubbard come right out onto the porch and she had a rifle and it was still smoking and she stood there, ready to shoot at me again."

Suddenly Hugh dropped the thumb from his vest pocket and leaned forward on the table, looking very serious.

"How close did those bullets come to you?"

"Why, them bullets like to of kilt me! Just singing right down there, next to my body, knocking holes in my boat. Why, the fright alone would of kilt a person who didn't have a strong constitution like mine!" Lumley sat straight up and looked righteous.

"Did you say anything to Mary Lou?"

"Nary a word. I just turned that boat like a flash and started for home. There I was, out to do my Christian duty when this poor hateful child tried to kill me. Tried to kill me, I tell you! I can still hear that rifle banging and those bullets singing and just missing me."

"Did you fear for your life?"

"Why, I just knowed I was dead, right there! I wasn't scared, I was terrified out of my wits. Anybody would have been with all them bullets smacking in there right by my body."

"Did you go directly home?"

"Yes. Well, no. What I done, I rowed as far as I could before that boat sank and then I swam the rest of the way. I was afraid she would shoot me across the river so I real quick run up the bank and never quit running 'til I got to the sheriff in Little Fork. I told him the story about how that hateful child tried to kill me and he wrote it all down and then he said he would have to take it to the governor because it happened on the Idaho side, and that was out of his territory."

Rapid, loud footsteps on the stairs brought all eyes to the corner of the room, where Becky's head appeard in the stairwell.

"Mama, Benny's got to do a wee-wee and he says he can't hold it no longer."

"Land a livin'," Clara said with a jerk of her head for emphasis, "I can't just jump up in the middle of this trial and come. You go take him on over to the outhouse. Be sure you help him aim so he don't hit the wall. Now go on, darlin'."

"I tried but he says he's scared without you."

"You tell him I said so. Now move along."

Obediently Becky turned and they heard her rapidly clump down the stairs and back outside.

Hugh's face became a total blank. In all his studies of the law, which were considerable, he had never heard of a trial being interrupted because a two-year-old had to do a wee-wee. He turned towards Clyde, waiting to see what he would do about such an interruption.

Clyde looked back at him, puzzled over the stunned expression on Hugh's face. "Go on, finish your questions," he said, as though nothing had happened.

Hugh swallowed and shook his head to make his brain start to function and continued. "Did the Governor do anything?"

"He surely did. He got aholt of the Idaho governor and said he would make Mary Lou come over to Montana for a trial if the Idaho governor didn't make a trial here."

"Thank you, Mr. Lumley. Now, your honor, I would like to ask the court if I could take the jury downstairs, to the east side of the courthouse. Er, building. As proof of what Mr. Lumley has claimed, he and I have raised the boat from the river bottom and brought it here today, at considerable expense and a great deal of trouble. I want the jury to see the bullet holes in the bottom of the boat."

Clyde reflected for just a moment. "That sounds fair enough. Everybody . . ."

Again thumping was heard in the stairwell, and Becky's head appeared.

"Never mind, Mama. Benny done it in his pants. I took 'em off and washed him good and rinsed the pants at the pump and hung 'em on the wagon, and he's running around with nothing on while he dries off. He's happy now."

"That's fine, Becky, now you go on and tend him."

This time Hugh didn't even flinch.

Clyde finished his sentence, " . . . move on downstairs and we'll have a look at the boat."

Five minutes later they were all gathered around the boat, gazing at six bullet holes. Stoically, Injun Charlie slowly reached his hand into the boat and laid it on the holes. It covered all six of them. He held it there until everyone saw, then raised it slowly and backed up, squeaking his pipe.

"Your honor, may I question Mr. Lumley about those holes?"

"Sure. Go ahead."

"Mr. Lumley, are those the holes you spoke of that sank your boat?"

"Them is the ones."

"Shot by Mary Lou Hubbard?"

A naked two-year-old cherub came careening around the corner as fast as two pudgy little feet would carry him and ran directly to the folds of Clara's skirt and hugged her leg. She patted him on his head and smiled.

"Yes sir," answered Lumley.

"How far did you estimate it was from where she fired the rifle to your boat, at the time she shot?"

"Oh, I figger seventy or eighty yards."

"Thank you. Your honor, if everyone is satisfied about the holes, would you care to take the jury back to the courtroom?"

"Anybody need to look at this boat and the holes any longer?" Clyde asked.

There were general head shakes and murmurings of no, except for Amos Two Fingers, who was heard to quietly say to Luke Tumfister, "Right smart shooting, even for Mary Lou."

Hugh heard it and turned to look at the two, wondering just what that meant.

When all had again taken their place in the courtroom, Hugh said, "I have no more questions of this witness. Defense counsel may cross examine."

It took Clyde a minute, but he figured that one out alone, and his eyes began to take on a look of confidence. "That means you, Injun Charlie. You want to ask Corvis any questions?"

The old Indian didn't move a muscle except to give his head one perfunctory shake, no.

"All right. Are you finished with Corvis then, Mr. Prosecutor?"

"I am finished."

"Lumley," said Clyde, "you get back over there by Mr. Prosecutor. Mr. Prosecutor, who do you want to witness next?"

Abner touched Clyde's arm and gave him a big wink of approval at how well he handled that.

Hugh looked down the table. At the far end, Mary Lou was leaning forward, her face turned towards him. She was smiling and there was a starry, dreamy look in her eyes. Her face was shining.

This was not the two-hundred-seventy-pound, six-and-a-half-foot Amazon with a rifle in one hand and an axe in the other he had been expecting. How could this beautiful, lovely, pristine, pure, simple mountain girl be an attempted murderess? Impossible. Not those limpid, trusting, sweet, appealing, innocent eyes. Never!

Legs spread wide, he lowered his head for a moment and decided. He could not continue one minute longer without knowing. "I now call Mary Lou Hubbard to testify."

Clyde said, "Mary Lou, come on around here and sit in the witness chair."

Mary Lou rose, her eyes never leaving Hugh. She floated slowly around the end of the table to the witness chair, never once allowing her gaze to be interrupted. Her rosebud mouth was curved up slightly, her cheeks flushed as she settled into the chair, her trim shape leaned slightly forward, hands clasped in her lap. Breathlessly she waited for the very first words Hugh Fitzgerald would speak to her directly.

11

"SWEAR AT HER, ABNER," CLYDE said, feeling the beginnings of a sort of general understanding of how all this was supposed to work.

"Raise your right hand, Mary Lou."

She mechanically raised her hand, still gazing at Hugh.

"You swear you're going to tell us the truth? All of it?"

She slowly nodded her head yes.

"Okay. She's swore at. Go ahead."

Hugh looked into her eyes and got lost in the two blue-violet pools for a second or two before he caught himself.

"State your name, please."

Mary Lou sighed. "Mary Lou Hubbard."

Suddenly old Lumley sat bolt upright and half raised from his bench. "Wait just a dang minute here. Where's Clarence? Mary Lou, where's Clarence?" he bellowed.

She said, "At home" without turning her head.

Lumley made a frantic lunge up and towards the stairwell. "He knows I'm here. He ain't home. He's on his way over to my place to do something rotten to get even for this here trial. That's where he is."

Clyde grabbed the hammer and whacked her down on the table a good one. "Order in this court. Lumley, you go back over and sit down or I'm going to contempt . . . . "

Lumley didn't stop. He hit the stairwell at a run and they could hear his boots whomping on the stairs as he bolted down two at a time and he was gone.

"Dang it, "Abner whispered, "you got to be quicker, Clyde. You missed your chance to contempt old Lumley."

"Cuss it all," Clyde whispered back, "I whacked the table a good one and I was contempting him when he ran out. Goldang it, I missed my chance. Goldang it!" He gritted his teeth in anger at his lost golden opportunity.

Still scowling at his own mistake, Clyde glanced at the old clock that was loudly ticking away the minutes and quickly brought his eyes back to Hugh.

"Go ahead with witnessing Mary Lou."

Hugh had hardly taken his eyes off her, despite the ruckus.

"Where do you live?"

"Off east a couple of miles, by the river."

"What is your age?"

"I'll be eighteen in August."

Suddenly Clyde ducked his head and whispered to Abner, "Wait a minute here. Didn't I read somewhere in that constitution paper that you can't make a person say things that are against themselves? Didn't I read that?"

"Might have," Abner allowed. "I don't rightly remember. Sounds right though. Sounds real American. If it ain't the law it oughta be."

"I think I read it."

"Well, do something about it!"

Clyde straightened and said abruptly, "Just a minute here. If you're going to make Mary Lou say things about herself that will be hurtful, then that ain't right. I object and I sustain the objection."

Hugh nodded his head, catching the hang of what Clyde said. "Your honor, I don't intend asking the defendant any questions that will be hurtful to her. I just want to ask her a few things about the day it all took place."

Clyde looked skeptical. "Well, maybe you can ask her a few things like that, but don't you get her confused and make her say things that she shouldn't ought to say."

Hugh said, "Thank you, your honor. Now, Mary Lou, how long have you known Corvis Lumley?"

"All my life."

"Do you recall the earliest time you can remember him?"

"When I was two or three. I remember Papa being real mad because he snuck some onions in the feed manger of our old cow and her milk went bad and we couldn't use it for two days."

"Do you dislike Corvis Lumley? Do you hate him?"

"Why, no." Her eyes grew large and earnest. "It ain't right to hate folks."

"How do you feel about him?"

"I feel kind of sorry for him. If he'd spend his time doing good things for folks, instead of mean ones, he would be a lot happier man."

"How do you feel about other people around the Settlement?"

"I feel fine about them."

"The young men? Do you feel fine about them?"

"Of course."

"Any one in particular?"

"No, just all of them."

Clyde ducked his head again and whispered, "Abner, what's going on here?"

Abner shook his head. "Thunderation, I think Fitzgerald is sweet on Mary Lou!"

Clyde's eyes widened and he straightened up, fumbling in his mind for how he should stop this. Hugh glanced at him and when he saw the expression on Clyde's face he turned quickly back to Mary Lou and changed his line of questions.

"On the day of the shooting, do you remember what happened?"

"Oh yes. It was me done the shooting. I remember real clear."

Hugh leaned slightly forward, his legs still wide apart, and gazed deeply into her eyes.

"Mary Lou, did you intend to murder Corvis Lumley that day?"

Clyde whacked the hammer down. "Now just a dang minute. Seems to me that could be a hurtful question."

"Why, your honor," said Hugh with his eyes wide and innocent, "that could only be hurtful if she meant to kill him."

"Well, she didn't," Clyde said.

"Then there can be no harm in her answer," said Hugh.

"Well, all right. But you be careful, Mr. Prosecutor."

"Indeed I will. Mary Lou, did you intend to murder Corvis Lumley that day?"

"Oh, no. I wouldn't hurt him." She was still smiling, her eyes still dreamy.

"Are you telling me you can shoot a heavy rifle well enough to put six shots within one hand span at eighty yards, on a downhill shot?"

"That's easy. 'Course."

Hugh recoiled, the disbelief apparent on his face. He took a breath to ask his next question and then stopped when they all heard footsteps in the stairwell. Nathan Jensen's head appeared, and wearing his best suit, with his hat in his hand, he stood at the top of the stairs.

"I'm sorry to be late. Where do I sit?"

"Right over there on the bench next to Clara," Clyde said, pointing. "Step right on over, we're going to be late."

As Nathan walked over, Clara said, "Which one fell in the well, Nathan? Are they all right?"

"Willie. He didn't fall, he jumped. We got him out and he's all right."

"Jumped?" asked Clara. "Mercy me, what for?"

"He just said he wanted to know where the water came from down there. Said he'd never been that far down to find out. I had to tie his hands together to get him out. He was figgering to stay down there until he found out."

"My, this new crop of kids," exclaimed Clara. "Sometimes they just wear a body out with their new ideas and nonsense. Why, my Barbara tried to fly off the chicken coop wearing some wings she made, and knocked her breath out so bad she turned blue. Eyes didn't come uncrossed for a week. Just wears a body out."

Nathan took his seat and turned dutifully towards Clyde.

Hugh blinked and blinked again when he realized what had happened.

"Your honor," he began, "is it the intention of this court to let Mr. Jensen take his place on the jury now, after Mr. Lumley has testified and left?"

Clyde said thoughtfully, "Yes, that's what this court intends."

"How will the new juror be able to help with the verdict if he did not hear what Mr. Lumley had to say?"

"Don't worry about that, Mr. Prosecutor. I told him most of it when I talked to him about coming, and what I missed, we can tell him later if we need to. Now we're getting real late so if you got any more questions to ask Mary Lou, you better get them asked."

Hugh shook his head, refusing to bother himself with an effort to unravel the snarl of how to handle the arrival of the new juror.

"Mary Lou, did you mean to place those shots that close to Mr. Lumley? Just barely miss him?"

"I meant to put them right where they hit. They weren't very close to him."

"Not very close? Right between his feet! Isn't that close? What would you have done if one had hit him?" The tone in Hugh's voice had become pleading, nearly frightened.

For the first time the smile disappeared from Mary Lou's face.

"Why, that would have been terrible. But there was really no danger of that. I hit where I shot."

"Thank heaven," Hugh muttered under his breath. Then to Mary Lou, "Why didn't you just go on down and tell him to go home if he landed at your boat dock?"

Her forehead wrinkled and she leaned forward and the expression on her face became serious.

"Because two or three times I heard him when Papa caught him on our place doing bad things and he ranted and raved and swore he would burn the place down if he ever got a chance, and I didn't want to let him do that. I knew I couldn't argue with him if he got riled so I knew I had to use the rifle to persuade him to go home."

Hugh heaved a sigh, more of relief than anything else. With the knowledge he had asked her questions not permitted under the law, he looked a little guilty and sat down.

"Your honor, I have no more questions to ask of Mary Lou."

Mary Lou looked at him as though she were pained, then dropped her eyes for a moment and raised them again. She was smiling and the dreamy look was back in her eyes.

"If you're finished, Mary Lou, you go back over and sit down where you were. Mr. Prosecutor, who else you got that you want to witness?"

"No one. We rest our case."

Clyde struggled for a moment with what that meant and then his face brightened and he said, "Well, then, I think it is Injun Charlie's turn."

Hugh Fitzgerald raised his head and started to place his hand on the table when he stopped all motion. His face was a mask, showing stark terror crossed with mortal fear.

Clyde studied him a second, then thrust his own face a little closer and looked at Hugh, who sat like a stone statue. Clyde slowly turned his head to see what had transfixed Hugh and his line of vision came to rest on Clara Peabody.

She had just unbuttoned the top button of her dress and was making ready to nurse little Glory, who was clutched to her bosom.

12

IN HIS LIFETIME, HUGH HAD NEVER
seen a mother nurse her young. He went numb and his face reddened. He could not move or close his mouth or quit staring. He
simply sat there, legs apart, hand frozen in midair, eyes wide, his
face a total blank.

"Here she comes, Glory. Just a minute and here she comes."
Clara leaned forward for a moment and Glory came searching and
little sucking sounds began and then stopped as Glory settled in her
mother's arms and began to draw.

"Mmmmmm, mmmmm," said Clara smiling through clamped
teeth. "That aches just a little before it feels good."

Everyone remained silent during the performance and as soon as
Glory was nursing, Clyde turned matter-of-factly back to the business at hand.

Still Hugh did not move. His eyes were glued to Glory, hugged
to Clara's ample bosom. He watched as Clara swayed gently forward and back just a little while Glory drew and tugged and flexed
her tiny fingers. The drawings of human anatomy he had studied in
biology at Harvard had included both male and female, but it was
perfectly obvious to him that whoever made the drawings had been

very selective in their source materials. They certainly had never seen Clara Peabody's anatomy while she was nursing little Glory! In the far reaches of the nether regions of his brain, Hugh caught his first signal that it was possible his education at Harvard had left one or two minor gaps.

Embarrassed clear to the soles of his feet, he furtively glanced around. Maudie was looking at Clara, envy written all over her face. Abner was whispering to Clyde, unconcerned about the nursing baby. Luke Tumfister was making a deal with Amos Two Fingers about moonshine. Nathan Jensen, sitting right next to Clara, glanced at the nursing baby and smiled, then began to twirl his hat nonchalantly in his hands, waiting for Clyde to go on. Hugh looked at Mary Lou, whose face showed supreme rapture as she watched Clara nursing the tiny soul.

Hugh licked his lips tentatively and waited for someone to say something about the nursing that would embarrass him. No one even noticed. He turned his head and looked around the room again. Everyone seemed to be perfectly at ease.

"Clara," Clyde said, "will you be all right with the baby?"

"Oh, mercy me, yes. Go right on, Clyde. You ain't going to disturb Glory and me."

"Good. Injun Charlie, it's your turn. If you got anyone to witness for Mary Lou, get them on the witness chair now. Abner, you swear at them."

Slowly Injun Charlie reached up and removed his pipe from the slit that served as his mouth. A hush settled as everyone expected him to say something. Without a word he stood and placed the pipe back between his teeth and started towards the stairwell, Mary Lou following right behind.

"Injun Charlie wants all of you to come on downstairs," she said. "He wants to show you something."

Clyde said, "Well, I guess everybody follows Injun Charlie."

He stood and everyone stood and they all walked downstairs, out into the sunlight on the east side of the building. Charlie walked over to his mule and drew a long blanket wrapped object from the saddle ties and reached into the inner folds of his shirt and brought out a handful of .30-30 cartridges. He walked back to Mary Lou and unwrapped the Hubbard family Winchester and handed the rifle and six cartridges to her.

Everyone watched as she tipped the rifle slightly in her left hand and in a couple of seconds had all six cartridges rammed into the loading port and faced Charlie, ready. Charlie motioned to Clyde to line everybody up behind Mary Lou, which they did, suspecting what was coming next. Then Injun Charlie reached into the folds of his shirt one more time and drew out six round, smooth river rocks about the size of robin's eggs.

Standing ten feet to one side of Mary Lou, he looked at her and she ran the action on the old rifle and gave him the nod.

He dropped his arm and with a quick upward swing arced the first rock up in the air forty feet. The rifle barely touched Mary Lou's shoulder before it cracked and the rock disappeared in a cloud of dust.

Injun Charlie dropped his arm again and Mary Lou ran the action as he arced two rocks in the same general direction as the first. She took the first one rising and the second one falling. She ran the action on the rifle and waited.

Hugh stood rooted to the ground, chin nearly on his belt buckle, hands clapped over his ears against the banging explosions, his eyes refusing to believe what they had seen.

Mary Lou nodded again. Injun Charlie's arm whipped and this time the last three rocks arced upwards together.

Mary Lou took the first one rising, the second at its peak, the third one falling. On each shot, everyone could hear the smack as the hurtling slug smashed the rock into dust. Then Mary Lou ran the action on the Winchester, closed the lever slowly while she watched the shell lifter to be certain no cartridge lifted into place to be driven into the firing chamber by the bolt, and closed the lever tight. She caught the hammer with her thumb, pulled the trigger, and lowered the hammer full down on the pin, then backed it off one click and handed the safe, empty rifle to Injun Charlie. The entire demonstration had taken just about ten seconds, first shot to last.

Hugh had moved only to raise his head watching the rocks. When the last cracking shot stopped echoing in the pines he slowly lowered his hands and stared at Mary Lou as though he were seeing someone from another world.

Injun Charlie rewrapped the rifle in the blanket and tied it back on the mule.

"Right smart shooting," Amos Two Fingers said to Luke Tumfister. "Looks like she hasn't lost her eye, what with growing up and all."

"Yep. Purty little thing like that, it's a surprise every time."

Injun Charlie led the processional back up to the courtroom and without a word sat down at his table.

The last one up the stairs and the last to take his place back at the table was Hugh. In his wildest contrivances he could not equate the calm, cool, deadly shooting he had just seen with the sweet, pure, innocent Mary Lou! He looked at her, seated up the table by Injun Charlie, and she was staring back at him as she had during the trial. Angelic, innocent, beautiful, a trace of smile lifting her rosebud mouth, the blue eyes mirrors of the purest of hearts.

"Well, Injun Charlie," Clyde said, "you want Mary Lou to sit in the witness chair and say anything?"

Injun Charlie squeaked his pipe once and gave his head a single shake, no.

"You got any more questions for Mary Lou, Mr. Prosecutor?"

"Your honor, do I understand Mary Lou is not going to take the witness chair in her own behalf? That shooting exhibition was the whole defense?"

A cloud crossed Clyde's face. "Injun Charlie, was that the whole defense?"

Injun Charlie gave his head one nod, yes.

"You got it all, Mr. Prosecutor. You got any more questions you want to ask Mary Lou?"

"No. I . . . no."

Clyde looked at the battered old clock, ticking away the minutes.

"It looks like we got about twenty more minutes. Maudie, you got things set up downstairs for when we're through?"

"I better go down and turn the roast once more and check those pies." She hurried to the stairwell and was gone.

Clyde leaned over and whispered to Abner, "What was that word you read about ending up a trial?"

"Summation. They each have a chance to make a summation. That means they can talk about the evidence and try to persuade the jury."

Clyde straightened and said, "Then I think we're down to giving the prosecutor and the defense counsel a little time to make up their summation. Now, that means they're going to tell the jury why they think Mary Lou is guilty or not guilty. On that point, I got to tell the jury, when you're through, you will have to make up your minds. If Nathan don't know enough about the facts to make up his, you others help him. When you all get your minds made up then you got to agree, and there are just two things you can agree on. Mary Lou is guilty or she is not guilty. There ain't no third choice. So when you got your minds made up you tell Abner and he'll tell me and we'll hear what you got to say."

He paused and studied the top of his table a minute, to be sure he had remembered it all, and satisfied, he looked at Hugh.

"All right, Mr. Prosecutor. You go first."

13

HUGH STOOD AND TRIED TO GATHER his thoughts. He glanced up the table at Mary Lou and she was smiling slightly, the entranced look still lingering on her face.

He swallowed hard, then was interrupted by Clara.

"You fussin', darlin'? Here. I thought I got the air out during the shooting, but I guess I didn't get it all." Gently she placed the infant on her broad shoulder and began to rub, then softly pat her tiny back.

Hugh looked at her big, round, homely face filled with love for everyone, then at the tiny infant on her shoulder. He thought about the prim, trim, proper blue-blooded ladies in Boston that gathered at his mother's afternoon tea socials for the sole purpose of out-dressing and outgossiping each other.

He drew another breath and was ready to begin when footsteps on the stairwell stopped him. Maudie walked to her place, sleeves rolled up, a wisp of hair curled in the perspiration on her forehead, smelling richly of venison roast, deep-dish apple and berry pies, mashed potatoes and peas and corn. She sat down and picked up her pencil, ready to finish. He looked at her for a moment and unexpected thoughts and memories came rushing. "Lay right down

there, sonny . . . got some doctorin' to do . . . spread them legs . . . I
seen more bare backsides than you seen dressed . . . here's some
dinner . . . you just stay right there until tomorrow . . . I'll point you
toward Lumley's . . ."

Maudie leaned back when she saw the strange look on his face, a
mix of reverence and shock.

Hugh looked up the table at Mary Lou once more. Small, a
jewel of natural grace and beauty, handle a Winchester like Annie
Oakley and Buffalo Bill combined. He looked at Clyde, suddenly
understanding the price he had paid to undertake this impossible
trial assignment.

What was happening? What was going on inside? What was
this odd, new feeling that was beginning to nudge him again and
again? Why did he feel a sad sorrow for the people home in
Boston, the proper people who led proper lives and died proper,
never having seen a Maudie or a Clara or a two fingered half-breed
who made moonshine, or an old hermit who set his own broken leg
and stumped twelve miles on a donkey to sit on a jury, or a Clara
with fifteen kids or a Maudie who seemed to be able to do anything?

He rallied. He reached deep and told himself he had his duty
and he was going to do it. He drew a great breath and turned his
face to the judge and waddled out in front of his table, facing
Clyde.

Maudie grinned to herself at his stance, shaking her head.
"Dang spunky little hummer," she said admiringly under her breath.

Hugh released his pent-up breath and began.

"Ladies and gentlemen of the jury, I must tell you, in many ways
this has been a very rare experience for me. I want to thank you all
for your attention and sharing this time with me."

Glory burped. The small explosion echoed in the huge room,
bringing every eye to the tiny bundle.

"Land a mercy, wouldn't you know," said Clara as she pulled the
baby from her shoulder and checked for spit-up, of which there was
a spot. She dabbed at it with Glory's blanket and settled the baby
down onto her lap and everyone looked to see. The little soul was
sound asleep.

"Go ahead, sonny, You won't bother her." Clara grinned her most comforting grin at Hugh.

A slow smile spread across Hugh's face. His head nodded slightly. "Thank you, Clara. I'll try to talk low."

Clara gave him a big wink.

"I was sent in here by Governor Potts to try this case, to see if Mary Lou Hubbard committed the crime of attempted murder when she fired the shots into the boat of Corvis Lumley. Old Lumley and I spent the whole day yesterday in the river finding that boat and it took two mules an hour to drag it ashore. Just like he said, there were six holes in the bottom of the boat, and there is no doubt Mary Lou Hubbard put them there."

Walking crabwise, Hugh took two strides towards the jury. "The question is, what did Mary Lou intend to do when she fired those shots? Lumley is dead certain she meant to kill him. He raved about it all day yesterday while I was diving in that river, tying ropes to the boat on the river bottom so we could pull it out to prove he was right.

"Mary Lou told us she sure enough did the shooting. But she says she put those bullets right where she meant to, and she absolutely did not mean to harm Lumley. Only make him go home and leave the Hubbard place alone.

"Now that brings us to the thing you will have to decide. Did Mary Lou tell us the truth, or did Lumley tell us the truth about what Mary Lou intended doing?"

Hugh stopped and scratched his head, then rubbed his smooth chin, and finally pulled his ear a little. Born of desperation and a growing, strong compulsion, the thoughts formed in his head as he spoke.

"So I have a proposition to put to you."

Everyone on the jury sensed it. He had found the way. The courtroom went silent and the noon sunlight poured through the windows. Hugh crabbed closer to the jury and his eyes swept theirs, one at a time. The air seemed charged as he began.

"Can a seventeen year old girl, who stands about five feet two inches and weighs about one hundred five pounds, take a Winchester .30-30 lever action rifle and at eighty yards fire six shots in six seconds and have them all strike a pattern no larger than a man's hand? Shooting down an incline into the bottom of a moving boat, near a man she fears?"

He stopped. Again his eyes probed each of theirs and he saw
what he was looking for in them and he felt a tingle.

"Why, of course not. No seventeen year old girl can shoot like
that! Can she? Naw, it's impossible! Mary Lou absolutely could
not shoot like that. And because Mary Lou Hubbard could not
shoot like that, she is obviously guilty!"

Hugh stopped and crabbed a step sideways. "Now," he said and
waited until every eye was on him, everyone focused, holding their
breath, "of course, if Mary Lou Hubbard *can* shoot like that, ..."
He let the sentence trail off, and his eyebrows raised as he waited
for each of them to complete the sentence.

The half-breed moonshiner, Amos Two Fingers, was the first to
grin. Then Luke, then Lee, his round, swarthy face looking like a
melon with two huge rows of teeth. Finally, old Gibbons and Clara,
who reached to tuck the blanket tightly around Glory.

Abner shook his head in admiration, then nudged Clyde.

Clyde shook his head to bring his thoughts back to his duties,
and gestured towards the counsel table.

"Injun Charlie, it's your turn."

At first everyone thought Injun Charlie had not heard. For several seconds he didn't move and Clyde had started to repeat it when
Injun Charlie reached up and drew his pipe from his set jaw.
Majestically he rose to his feet. His eyes glowed like chips of black
flint, and his face turned slowly to Mary Lou, his huge hawk nose
giving his craggy old face a fierce appearance, like an eagle.

The room grew still as a tomb. Hardly anyone had ever heard
Injun Charlie speak. Some didn't believe he could. No one
breathed as they waited.

He opened his mouth and spoke in deep tones that seemed quiet
but rumbled out to pierce every corner of the room.

"If little sister mean to kill Lumley, he be dead."

And Injun Charlie set his pipe back in his teeth and sat down
with pride.

Instantly, murmuring and open talk broke out all across the
room. Maudie said, "Well, if that don't beat all!"

With sounds that overrode all other sounds and filled the room,
Glory's face went red and all scrooched up and she grunted until

her tiny neck veins stood out and everyone heard the muffled sound of a diaper being filled.

"Well, well, don't that feel just fine," Clara said as the happy child relaxed and smiled and looked relieved.

"Here, we'll fix that right now."

Expertly Clara removed the diaper, grabbed the tiny ankles and wiped everything clean and dropped the messed one in with the last of the clean ones. In a moment she had the child on her shoulder, and again turned to face Clyde.

"Just go right on, Clyde. Glory's fine."

The room was suddenly filled with chatter as everyone on the jury began talking to everyone else. Abner leaned and whispered something to Clyde, and Clyde grabbed the hammer and whacked her down with a thump on the table.

"Order in the court. We got about three minutes until noon. Maudie, you go down and get set to feed this here court. Now you people on the jury, you go over to that corner and make up your minds, and when you know what you all think, you pick one to speak for all of you and come back and tell us. Go now."

"Hold on a minute there," Abner cut in. "I got some official clerking to do. After we eat, Maudie, you and I got to set down and make up an official judgment in this case, whatever that is. So you come back up here soon as the dishes is done." Abner sat back down, signaling he was finished.

The jury moved over to the corner and five seconds later Clara led them back to their bench.

"We got our mind made up and I'm to speak for the group. We have decided . . ."

"Now, hold on, Clara," Clyde cut in. "We got to do this proper. I'm supposed to ask you. You don't just come over and say it. So I'm asking you. Did you reach a verdict, guilty or not gilty?"

"Of course we did, Clyde, like I told you."

"All right, then, you tell it to Abner and Abner tells it to me. So tell Abner."

Everyone jumped as the old alarm clock started clanging.

"Goldang it," Clyde exploded, "we're too late. We're past noon. Now it aint going to be a legal verdict."

"Yes it is," countered Abner. "The minute hand is bent, if you'll remember, and by the clock we still got about a minute and a half."

"Quick, then," Clyde spat, "Clara, tell Abner."

Clara turned towards Abner. "Abner, we find Mary Lou not guilty."

"All right, Abner, now you tell me."

Abner turned towards Clyde and said, "Your honor, the jury decided Mary Lou ain't guilty."

"I suspected that. All right, then it is official. Mary Lou Hubbard is not guilty. What time is it?"

"We got about half a minute."

Clyde motioned desperately for Abner to lean over, whch Abner did.

"What was that dang word for us to quit? I forgot it."

"Adjourn. Say we adjourn."

Clyde raised up and said in a real loud voice, "And we adjourn."

"And whack the hammer," Abner whispered loudly. So Clyde whacked the hammer.

The clock said exactly noon. It was over.

Instantly Clara started for the stairwell with Glory cuddled against her bosom. "Now I got to git downstairs to help Maudie, and Mary Lou better come too. Feeding this crowd is going to take all three of us. Where's Becky? She's got to watch Glory."

The two women started for the stairwell and the men all started talking at once. Hugh stood and smiled to himself and then smiled some more and heaved a sigh. He felt good. He started for the stairwell, all alone.

"Hey, sonny, where you going?" Old Luke Tumfister stared at him, waiting.

"I'm through here. I thought I better just get back on my way to Boise to make a report."

"Well, you sure ain't going without you eat with us first. Now you just stick around for a spell, you hear?"

Lee shuffled over towards Hugh. "You come. Eat ham. Pie. Plenty pie." His round face, topped by his funny upside-down hat, shined and he had the biggest, toothiest grin Hugh had ever seen.

"Wait a minute," Hugh said. "I came here to send Mary Lou to prison. I didn't think you folks would be very kindly about that."

"Nonsense," said Abner. "You come to do a trial and you done a right fine job of it. You stick around for this feed."

Hugh looked at them, startled, unbelieving. They started for the stairwell in a herd and Amos Two Fingers dropped a friendly arm over Hugh's shoulder and drew him into the crowd and said, "Now, that sumpsion you made there at the last, where you got to just talk to us on the jury - that was some pretty good thinkin', for a city boy."

Hugh looked at him to see if he had been insulted, and Amos grinned at him and winked, and Hugh smiled back.

Old Gibbons reached over and whacked Hugh on the back and said, "Right smart, that was. Well, anyway, come on. You ain't really et until you et some of Maudie's venison ham and pie."

14

NEVER HAD HUGH SEEN ANYTHING like it! The table was out in the shade on the south end of the place, with settings for everyone, including Clara's kids. The red-and-white checkered tablecloth gleamed in the bright June sun.

Two huge platters of sliced venison ham roast were steaming, with bowls of fluffy mashed potatoes, gravy, peas, corn, yams, berries, nuts, and pitchers of fresh milk, water and apple cider dispersed throughout. At one end, on a small separate table, were six huge, deep dish pies, three apple and three blueberry.

The day was as lovely as the first day of creation. Birds chattered, chipmunks ventured as close to the rich, pungent aromas as they dared, and the Peabody children stood around, eyes wide, waiting for the signal from Clara. Little Benny was still without clothes, and Clara signaled Becky to put his pants back on him, since they were now dry.

Talking and laughing, everyone drifted to the table and found a place on the benches, and Maudie stood at the head.

"You're all welcome here as the sunshine. We better get into this food while it's still hot. Being the one in charge of this here meal, I'll call on someone to say grace."

Everyone fell silent.

"Abner, you're the one."

She bowed her head and everyone bowed theirs, and Abner raised his face to heaven, closed his eyes, and in his best voice said loudly, "Lord, we're right thankful for these victuals and the hands that prepared it. Bless the drink and bless the meat. Amen." Then he dropped his eyes to the silent table and quickly added, "Throw back yer ears and start to eat."

Everyone raised their heads with a grateful "amen" and instantly the air was filled with excited chatter. Pass this, pass that, excuse me, watch yer elbow, Benny keep them pants on, this meat is straight from heaven, how long was that cider in the cellar? - one year you say? - how did you whip them spuds so fluffy, where did you get those berries this time of year, pass some more of that cider - and on and on. Bits of laughter punctuated the spontaneous talk, and occasionally an out-and-out guffaw.

Hugh was seated between Lee and Amos Two Fingers and across the table was Abner. Hugh ate two helpings of everything, all the while getting an education in the art of distilling top-grade moonshine, Amos and Abner both seeming to be masters. Lee just nodded his head vigorously when anyone spoke to him and kept shoveling venison and potatoes into his ever-smiling mouth.

The heaping bowls and platters steadily emptied and the crowd at the table steadily filled. Nathan Jensen finally leaned back and patted his middle with both hands.

"I can still chew but I'm having trouble swallowing," he said.

Luke Tumfister blew his breath out through rounded lips and said, "That sure beats eating your own cooking, let me tell you. Been a spell since I et such victuals."

Maudie looked alarmed. "You better have enough room left down there for a piece of that pie."

"I'm eating a piece of that pie even if there ain't room," Nathan allowed, and those that were finished rose from the table and walked to the end where the pies were waiting, still warm.

When his turn came, Hugh held out his plate and Maudie asked which kind, apple or blueberry, and while he was trying to decide, she plopped a healthy slice of each on the plate and Hugh smiled his thanks.

Right behind Hugh came Mary Lou and she chose blueberry, and Hugh thought, just the color of her eyes. When they went back to the table the people didn't go back to their regular places, just sat on the benches backwards and held their plates while they ate the pies lovingly, working each mouthful thoroughly, talking little, savoring the pure ambrosia Maudie had created.

Mary Lou found herself sitting beside Hugh, and when their eyes locked over blueberry pie, they got lost. They ate pie and talked and grinned and then ate some more pie.

All too soon it slowed and then it was over. The piles of dirty dishes and depleted bowls and platters were scattered over the entire table. Reluctantly, one at a time, members of the group allowed as how they had better get back to their business, and started to rise, asking Maudie how they could help.

The dirty dishes were carried inside Maudie's store and placed in a huge tub of steaming water. The extra food was gathered into some heavy copper bowls, along with the meat that was left, and put in the bottom of Clara's wagon, covered with gunny sacks to keep it warm on the trip home.

"That aint necessary," protested Clara, but Maudie insisted and Benny and Buddy and Becky stood with anxious eyes until Clara consented, and Maudie told Becky to remember to bring the kettles back next trip, and Becky promised. Maudie got Clara aside for just a few minutes and they talked in low tones and just once, Maudie pointed at Hugh.

Before Luke Tumfister mounted his donkey for the ride back to his mine he paused to thank Maudie, and then shook Clyde's hand and said, "That was a real fine American trial," and waved to everyone as he turned the donkey northwest, while the bottom of the splint on his leg dragged a little in the dust.

"Hugh, you better come here a minute," Maudie called, "and Clara, I need your advice."

Mary Lou looked inquiringly, hoping to share in whatever it was if it concerned Hugh, but Maudie shook her head no, smiling the whole time.

Hugh crab-walked over and Maudie pointed inside and said, "Come on in here for a minute. I got to see what shape you're in."

This time, an understanding smile twitching at his mouth, Hugh walked over behind the sheet, followed by the two women, unbuck-led his belt and lowered his trousers and turned his back to them.

The women leaned over a little and inspected.

"Well," Clara opined, "that river water sort of helped yesterday, looks like, but if I was to say, I wouldn't be thinking about letting him travel over to Leadore for two, maybe three days. Keep some salve on those legs and be careful and it will probably heal all right."

"That's how I see it too," Maudie said matter of factly and whacked him easy on the behind, friendly, and smiled and said, "Pull up your drawers. You're staying on here for two or three days until that heals proper. And there ain't no arguing with that, do you hear?"

Hugh pulled up his trousers and turned slightly, grinning, and said, "I hear."

Maudie grinned from ear to ear. "Good. Now, things can get sort of monotonous around here after a while and what you don't need is a good case of cabin fever. So maybe you can ride around in a wagon or something and see some of the country. 'Course that might require someone who knows the country to see you get to the right places. Maybe Mary Lou can handle that."

Hugh shook his head, looking at these two lumpy, large women who at that moment were leaning slightly forward, waiting for his response.

"Maybe she can," he said and instantly both women grinned from ear to ear and turned.

"Well, better get back to the work," said Clara, and Maudie said, "Nonsense, you get that wagon moving back home. You'll be sun-set getting there now, so git going. You got enough food you won't have to prepare supper. Now you git."

Clara protested but Maudie hollered for Becky and Buddy to round up the kids, and Clara and her brood clambered up into the wagon seat. Benny gigged the horses and the wagon rumbled out of the clearing with Clara and the kids waving, and everyone wav-ing them out of sight.

Nathan Jensen swung out in a rapid walk with Lee shuffling along beside him, and Maudie called after him, "Now Nathan, you keep Willie away from that well, hear?"

"I hear. Thanks again, Maudie."

Amos Two Fingers shook Clyde's hand and waved and hollered his thanks again to Maudie, and he was gone, glancing furtively into the pines as always, looking for government revenuers who might be interested in finding his whiskey still.

Maudie stood with hands on her hips, watching them disappear, then turned back to the table and surveyed what was left to do.

"Well, it was sure one of the most interesting mornings I can remember in these parts," she said with a sigh. "Sort of too bad it has to end."

She began gathering up the tablecloth and Mary Lou came over and without a word started gathering the six empty pie tins off the smaller table, carefully throwing the crumbs onto the ground for the birds and chipmunks, who instantly came from hiding to claim them.

"Maudie, Hugh says you might want him to stay around a while, so he can heal. Is that true?"

"He's staying," Maudie said, like it was all settled.

"And he said he might need someone to take him around in the wagon so he can see some of the country."

"He sure does. And that's you."

Mary Lou hugged Maudie and murmured, "Thank you."

Clyde stretched and said, "Well, Abner, I better head back on out to my diggins. You send that black robe back to the governor. Maudie, how much are you going to charge for this banquet you served?"

"Oh, I don't know. Served about eighteen or twenty of us. Suppose twenty dollars would be too much?"

"Shall I put in for twenty? Governor's going to pay it."

"That ought to be enough. Think he'll pay it?"

"I don't know. I think I'll put in for twenty-six dollars. Them pies was worth an extra dollar each. Maybe Abner better hold that robe here until you get the money."

Abner nodded his head. "Can't trust them dang politicians."

"Oh, one more thing," Clyde continued. "You and Abner write up something and call it a judgment, saying Mary Lou was found not guilty. I'll come in a day or two and sign it and we'll send it on to the governor and attorney general."

Abner looked at Maudie and she nodded and it was settled.

Clyde turned to start the walk home, then stopped and walked back to Abner.

"Abner, thank you. You done real good as a clerk. Wearing that robe and all, you done real good. We wouldn't of got that trial over without you."

Abner blushed and his grizzled old Adam's apple bobbed.

"That wasn't nothing, Clyde. You was the one done the judging and you done it right smart, like you was borned to it."

They shook hands as Hugh walked up to them. Hugh's face was glowing and he thrust out his slender, strong young hand to Abner first, then Clyde.

"I want to shake the hands of two of the finest jurists I ever met."

Clyde looked at Abner and Abner whispered, "Jurist means we was in the judging business." Clyde grinned his relief. Hugh chuckled.

"You both served your state well," Hugh continued. 'I'll see to it the attorney general and governor hear about it. I was honored to have been allowed to serve with you."

Clyde blushed and then bobbed his head and said, "It was us who got honored. We are indebted to you for what you done. I hope to see you again some day and in the meantime, God bless you, Mr. Prosecutor."

"Hugh," Hugh said.

"God bless you, Hugh." Clyde's eyes dropped, and not knowing what else to say, he waved and was on his way to his diggins to check on his university grant seed experi- ment. He still could not figure out what was starting to grow in those last three lots.

He looked back just once, to see Abner and Maudie standing side by side, Hugh and Mary Lou beside them, standing very close to each other as they all waved.

15

"YOUR MORNING MAIL, SIR." ALFRED
Atchley Ambrose Humble set the silver tray down on the side of the
huge dark oak desk, his head held rigid, nose high.

Governor Cornelius Potts scratched his backside while he eyed
the stack. The top envelope was the largest, and he saw instantly it
was from the attorney general. Anxiously he snatched it and fum-
bled with the papers while he said, "What's Dingel got to say?"

"I do not look at official . . ."

"Can it, Al. What's Dingel saying?"

"The trial of Mary Lou Hubbard in the northern reaches of
Lemhi County is completed."

Potts stopped scanning the papers and said in strained tones,
"Well, let's have it."

"The jury found her not guilty."

Potts threw the papers on the desk and shouted, "Hallelujah, I
knew it. I knew it. What else did he say?"

"Mr. Dingel, or Mr. Fitzgerald?"

"Who's Fitzgerald?"

"He's the stout lad they sent in to prosecute the case for the
state, sir. Brilliant lad. He made a full report."

"Where is young Fitzgerald right now?"

"He resigned the day after he arrived back here, sir. Mentioned something about going back over to the Settlement with intentions of doing some serious courting of the defendant. Also, to learn more about the first 'honest to Heaven people' he had met in his life. He is gone."

A slow grin spread over Potts' face. "Darned sensible kid. Darned sensible. What did Fitzgerald have to say about the trial?"

"Most complimentary, sir. Seems the judge you selected, Mr. Clyde Dinwoody, did a masterful job of selecting a clerk, a reporter, and a jury. Fitzgerald's description of these characters was, to say the least, colorful."

Potts was delighted. "So Dinwoody got it done. He got it done. Go on."

"The court convened on the second floor of the historic Cataldo Mission."

"The old mission?" the Governor chortled. "Why, that thing has been shot at by everybody who passed through the country since 1600. I figured it was junk a long time ago."

"It was rather rustic, sir," Humble continued.

"Well, go on, go on, don't stop now," the Governor said, his eyes shining.

"Mr. Fitzgerald said all formalities of usual procedures were abided, save and except one or two which were of no consequence."

"Such as what?," the governor asked expectantly.

"Well, they could not find twelve jurors so they made do with six. The judge was embarrassed about wearing the robes so the clerk wore them. The judge appointed a Blackfoot Indian about eighty-five years old, more or less, to be defense counsel. The man said exactly ten words during the entire trial. The judge also interviewed the defendant rather closely three days before the trial, to determine whether she was guilty or not, then informed each of the jurors of his discussions and his conclusions when he invited them to be on he jury."

Potts whacked his thigh and his belly shook with his laughter.

"One of the jurors was of Chinese extraction, another was a hermit who came with a broken leg in a cast which he himself had arranged. Another was late because his son Willie had jumped into the family well to see where the water came from. One juror was

an infamous, er, - bootlgger, I believe you call them, named Amos
Two Fingers, of Caucasian and Indian ancestry. Another was a feed
store operator and the last was a woman who is the mother of fifteen children, five of whom she brought to the trial with her."

Potts was roaring.

"In the middle of the trial, said woman found it necessary to
nurse her four-month-old infant, which proved quite educational to
Mr. Fitzgerald when she produced the necessary equipment and the
little soul availed herself. Oh, I might also add, the nursing incident
was preceded by an occurrence in which the trial was interrupted
when little Benny had to do a wee-wee, which he eventually did in
his pants. It was later interrupted again when the infant evacuated
her bowels, noisily, in her diaper."

Potts was leaning forward in his chair, battling for breath.

"Mr. Corvis Lumley, the Montanan who made the charges to
begin with, testified of the foul deed done by Mary Lou Hubbard,
in great detail. He and Mr. Fitzgerald had gone through the
Herculean task of fetching the boat from the river bottom, and
brought it to court to prove the shooting. There were six holes in
the boat bottom, just as he had described them, all within one hand
span."

Potts eyes were bugging out, his face red, wheezing.

"The Indian who served as defense counsel, Injun Charlie as I
recall, put on a totally wordless defense by simply taking Mary Lou
Hubbard out behind the courthouse and letting her shoot six small
stones he flung into the air, in six seconds, more or less. It con-
vinced the jury that if Mary Lou had intended killing Mr. Lumley,
he would indeed have been dead with six bullets straight through
his heart."

"Al, stop, stop," Potts wheezed. "I can't take any more of this."

"I'm nearly through, sir," Humble continued. "The jury took
less than ten seconds to deliberate and found the young lady not
guilty."

Potts was pounding the table with his fists in an attitude of beg-
ging for mercy.

"And finally, sir, the entire trial took exactly three hours, from
nine a.m. until noon, the arrival of which was announced by the
clanging of an ancient alarm clock on which the minute hand had
been bent two minutes' worth. Seems the constitutional provision
that a defendant be afforded a speedy trial prompted the judge to

conclude that a trial commenced at nine a.m. and concluded by high noon should meet the requirements, and he saw to it they started, and stopped, on time."

Potts howled. He slapped the desk, then his thigh, then battled for air and his gales of laughter stopped people in the halls for one hundred feet each direction.

Humble cracked a smile and waited.

When Potts finally wiped away the tears that were streaming down his face and caught enough wind to allow the normal color to return to his pudgy face, he tried to gather his thoughts.

"Did they send a bill? What were expenses?"

"Twenty six dollars."

"WHAT?"

"Twenty six dollars."

"What for?"

"To induce the jurors to come to the trial judge Dinwoody promised them a free meal. The total cost of the meal was twenty six dollars."

"Who did they feed?"

"Everyone in the courtroom except Corvis Lumley, who took his leave abruptly during the trial when he discovered that Mr. Hubbard was not present in the courtroom, and suspected he was on the Montana side doing something disreputable to Lumley's place, out of an attitude of revenge for forcing the trial."

Potts broke into laughter and then pulled it under control.

"No jurors' fees, no court costs, no claim for pay for the judge nor the clerk nor the reporter for mileage allowance nor hotel costs? No nothing? Just the noon meal?"

"That is correct, sir. They thought it to be their patriotic American duty. Pay did not enter their minds."

"WHAT?"

"It was never once discussed nor mentioned, sir."

"They aint got their hand out asking for government money, even when they got a right?"

"That is correct, sir."

"Well, by thunder, that is going to be in the newspapers everywhere I can get it," Potts said emphatically. "Anything else, Al?"

"No sir, not to my immediate recall."

"Good. Al, you write out a letter to Governor Buggs and you make a thorough report on all this to him, for me to sign. Make sure you tell him how they did it all legal, and how we sent over our best man to prosecute that girl. I wouldn't include too much detail about the local gentry over there, not that it ain't good, but the legalities is what Buggs is after. So make sure it all sounds legal. Do you understand?"

"Perfectly, sir."

"Thank you, Al. Now I think I'll spend some time and read this report clear through. Don't let anybody in until I'm finished. All right?"

"Very good, sir."

Potts sat down and Humble started for the door when suddenly Potts stood, great agitation showing in his face.

"Al, wait a minute." He paced back and forth for a moment, then leaned against his desk and thrust a finger towards Humble, his sure sign of having received one of his frequent inspirations.

Humble paused, knowing something profound was coming.

"Al, bottom line, this judge - Dinwoody - did I understand he got this case tried in half a day?"

"Correct, sir."

"Twenty-six bucks total cost? That's it?"

"Correct, sir."

"Got the right result?"

"Not guilty. Correct, sir."

"Attorney general's office satisfied?"

"Delighted, sir."

"You dead certain about this twenty-six bucks?"

"I have already ordered the draft to be sent to 'Maudie,' sir."

Potts' hand jumped to his jowl and began to rub it slowly, then more vigorously, and Humble waited, knowing he was about to hear the conclusion of Potts' revelation.

"Al, do I remember right? Have we got a vacancy coming on the state supreme court next October when old Judge Hossfelder retires? Have I got that right?"

"That is correct, sir." Humble waited for a moment and suddenly the implication of Potts' question struck into his brain. His eyes widened and his thoroughly British demeanor was lost in a wide-eyed look of shock, bordering on terror.

"You wouldn't sir!" His head thrust forward and his mouth fell open as he saw the look in Potts' eyes.

"Oh, my sainted Aunt! You would!"